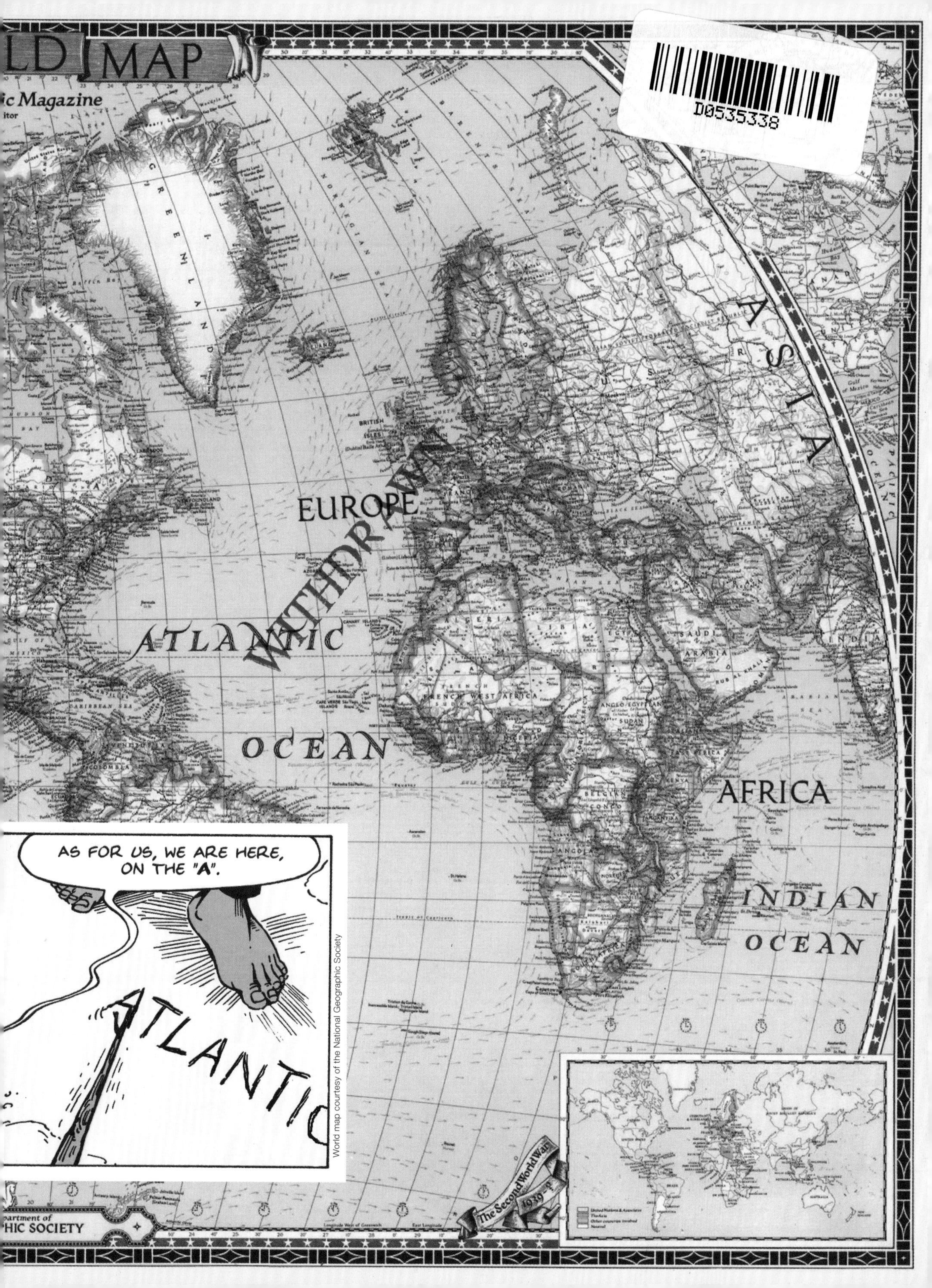
LD MAP
ic Magazine
ASIA
EUROPE
ATLANTIC
OCEAN
AFRICA
INDIAN
OCEAN
BRITISH ISLES
SAUDI ARABIA
FRENCH WEST AFRICA
ANGOLA
The Second World War
partment of
PHIC SOCIETY
AS FOR US, WE ARE HERE, ON THE "A".
ATLANTIC

World map courtesy of the National Geographic Society

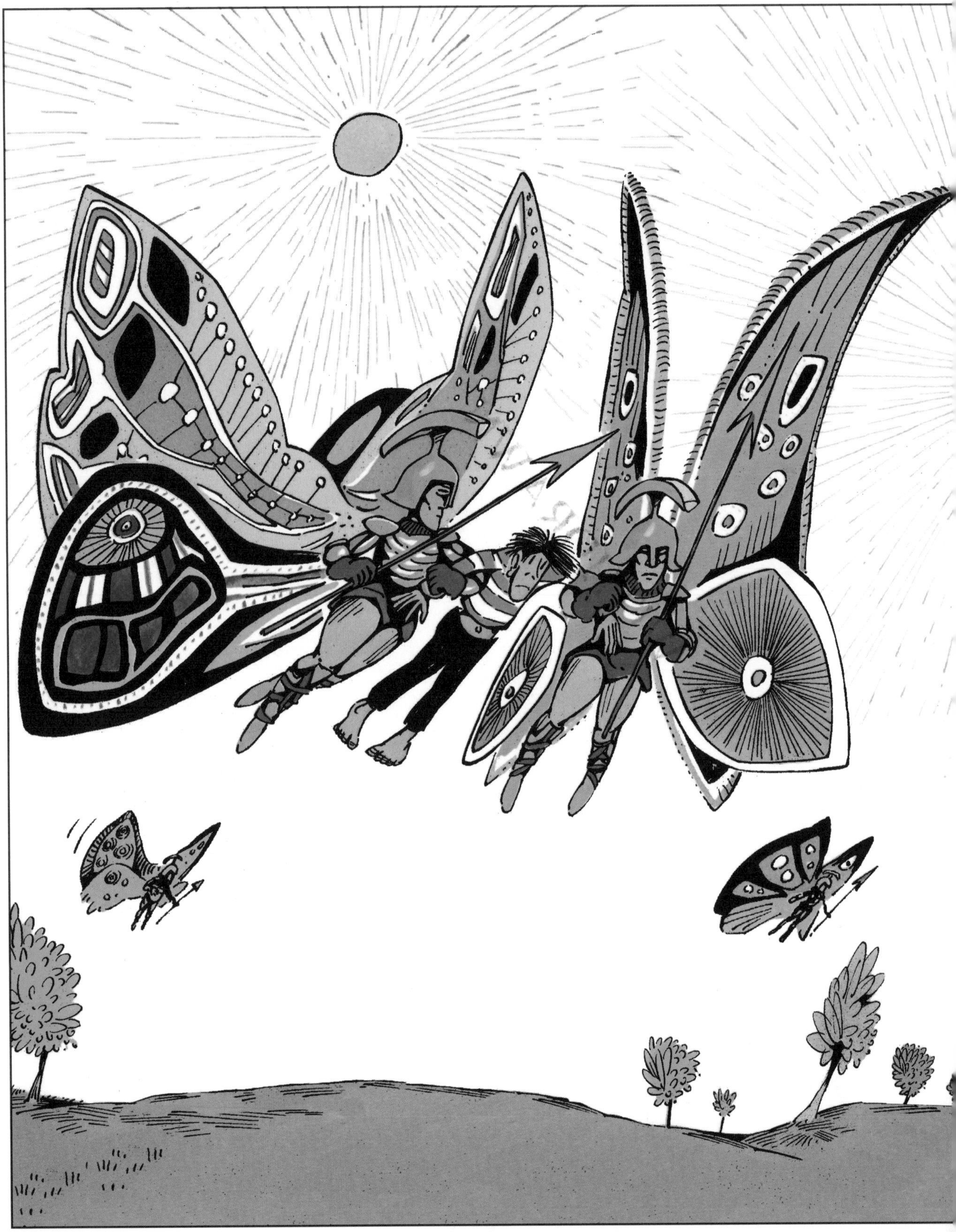

FRED

THE WILD PIANO

A PHILEMON ADVENTURE

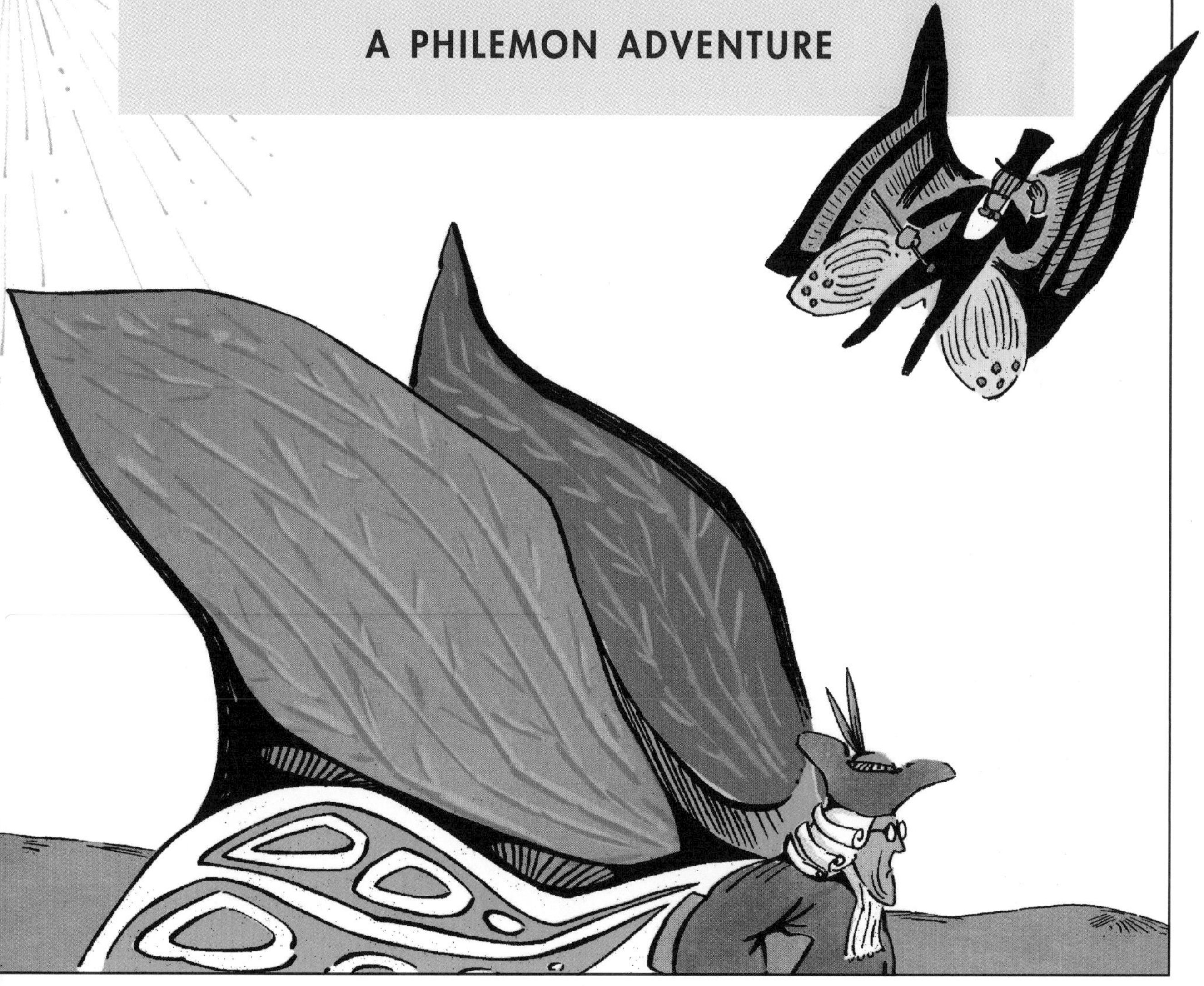

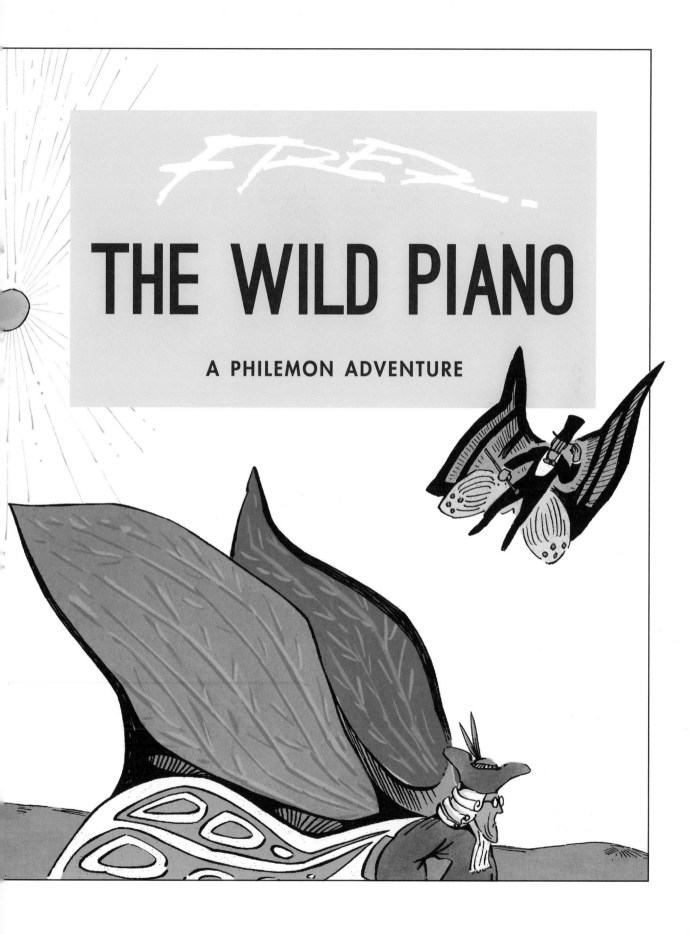

Editorial Director & Book Design: F R A N Ç O I S E M O U L Y

Translation: R I C H A R D K U T N E R

Hand-lettering: M Y K E N B O M B E R G E R & F R E D

F R E D ' S artwork was drawn in India ink, watercolor, and gouache.

FOR VISUAL READERS

TOON
GRAPHICS

A TOON Graphic™ © 2015 TOON Books, an imprint of RAW Junior, LLC, 27 Greene Street, New York, NY 10013. Original text and illustrations from *Philémon et le piano sauvage*, © 1973 DARGAUD. Translation, ancillary material, and TOON Graphic™ adaptation © 2015 RAW Junior, LLC. No part of this book may be used or reproduced in any manner whatsoever without written permission except in the case of brief quotations embodied in critical articles and reviews. TOON Graphics™, TOON Books®, LITTLE LIT® and TOON Into Reading!™ are trademarks of RAW Junior, LLC. All rights reserved. All our books are Smyth Sewn (the highest library-quality binding available) and printed with soy-based inks on acid-free, woodfree paper harvested from responsible sources. Printed in Shenzhen, China by Imago. Distributed to the trade by Consortium Book Sales and Distribution, Inc.; orders (800) 283-3572 34; orderentry@perseusbooks.com; www.cbsd.com.

Library of Congress Cataloging-in-Publication Data:

Fred, 1931- author, illustrator.   [Philémon et le piano sauvage. English]   The wild piano : a Philemon adventure / by Fred; translated by Richard Kutner.   pages cm. -- (The Philemon Adventures)   Originally published in French by Dargaud in 1973 under title: Philémon et le piano sauvage.   Summary: "Determined to save his friend the well digger from the labyrinth on the second 'A,' Philemon returns to the parallel world of islands that form the words 'Atlantic Ocean.' He finds himself on the 'N' where he inadvertently breaks the law, goes on trial, and is sentenced to confront the wild piano"-- Provided by publisher.

ISBN 978-1-935179-83-2   1. Graphic novels. [1. Graphic novels. 2. Adventure and adventurers--Fiction. 3. Islands--Fiction. 4. Alphabet--Fiction.]   I. Kutner, Richard, translator.   II. Title.   PZ7.7.F73Wi 2015   741.5'944--dc23   2014028860

ISBN 978-1-935179-83-2 (hardcover)

15 16 17 18 19 20 IMG 10 9 8 7 6 5 4 3 2 1

THE WILD PIANO

A PHILEMON ADVENTURE

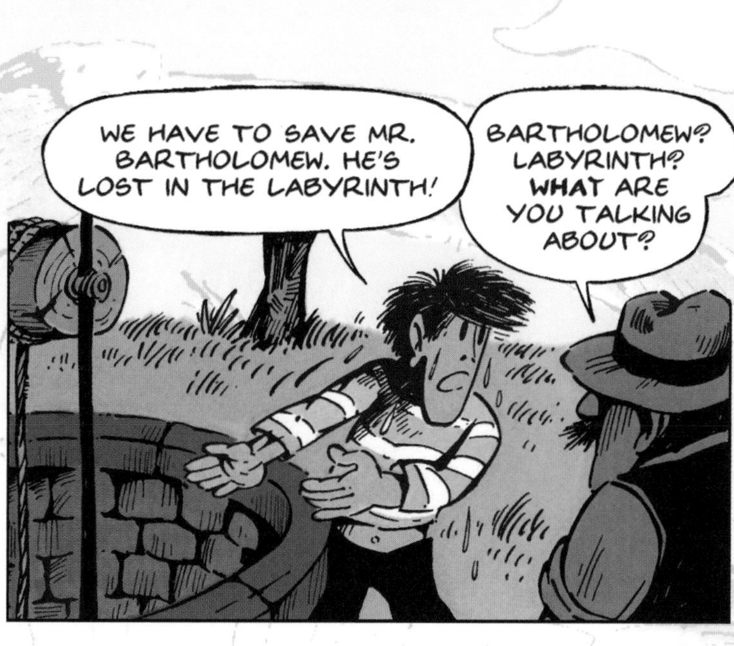
WE HAVE TO SAVE MR. BARTHOLOMEW. HE'S LOST IN THE LABYRINTH!
BARTHOLOMEW? LABYRINTH? WHAT ARE YOU TALKING ABOUT?

A TOON GRAPHIC BY

FRED

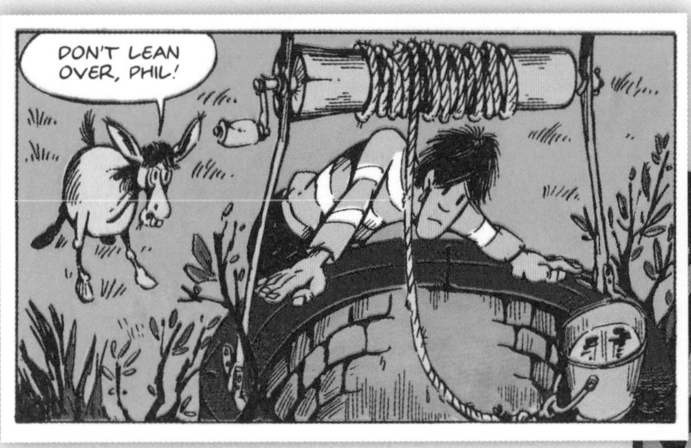
DON'T LEAN OVER, PHIL!

MEET PHILEMON

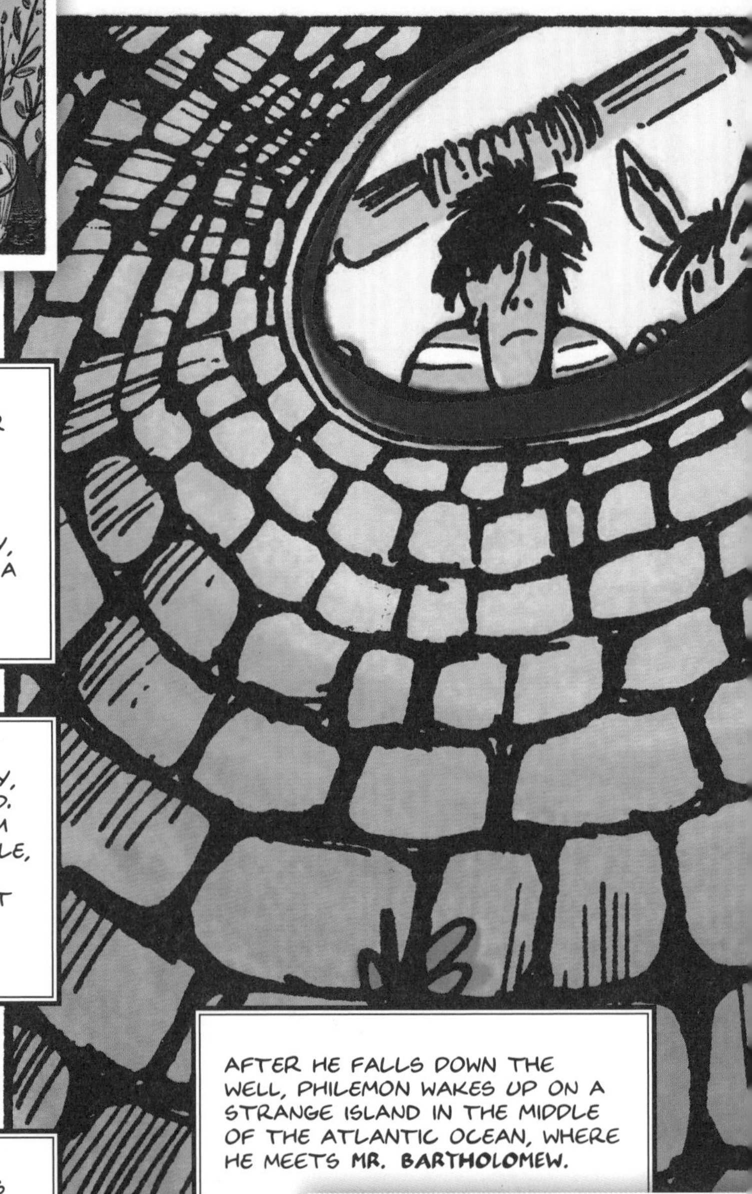

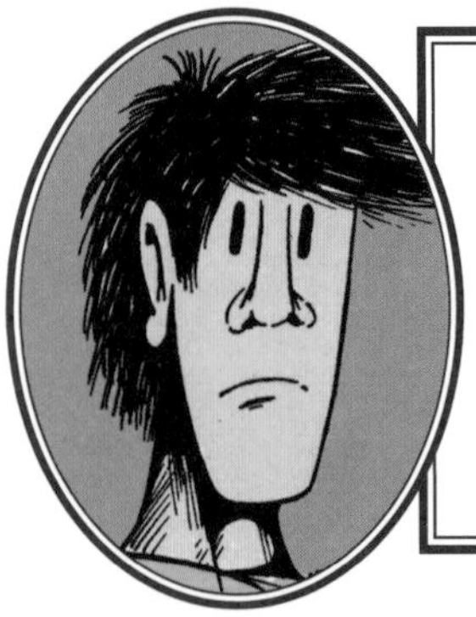

PHILEMON IS AN IMAGINATIVE TEENAGER WHO LIVES ON A FARM IN FRANCE, BACK IN THE 1960S. WHEN A MESSAGE IN A BOTTLE SPARKS HIS CURIOSITY, HE FALLS RIGHT INTO A WORLD OF FANTASTIC ADVENTURES...

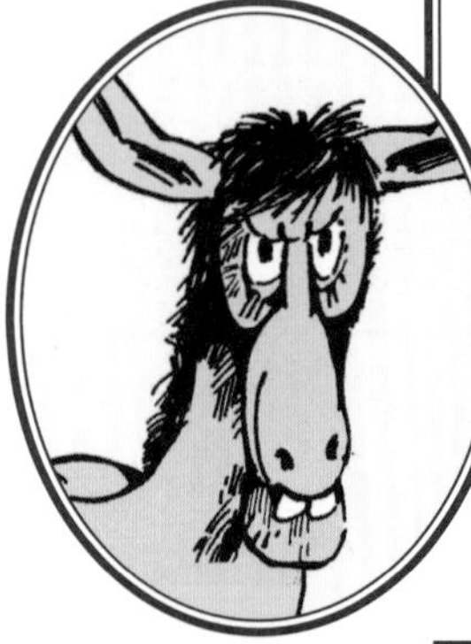

ANATOLE IS A DONKEY, PHIL'S TRUSTY FRIEND. HE TRIES TO HELP HIM STAY OUT OF TROUBLE, BUT PHILEMON'S ADVENTUROUS SPIRIT AND CURIOSITY GET THE BEST OF HIM.

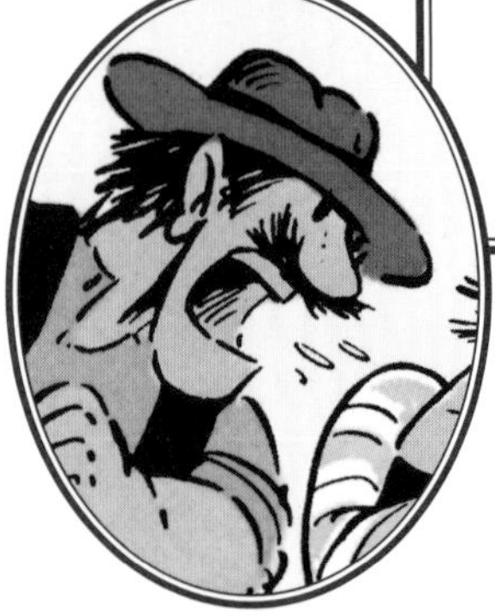

HECTOR IS PHILEMON'S GROUCHY FATHER, WHO REFUSES TO BELIEVE PHIL'S WILD STORIES.

AFTER HE FALLS DOWN THE WELL, PHILEMON WAKES UP ON A STRANGE ISLAND IN THE MIDDLE OF THE ATLANTIC OCEAN, WHERE HE MEETS **MR. BARTHOLOMEW.**

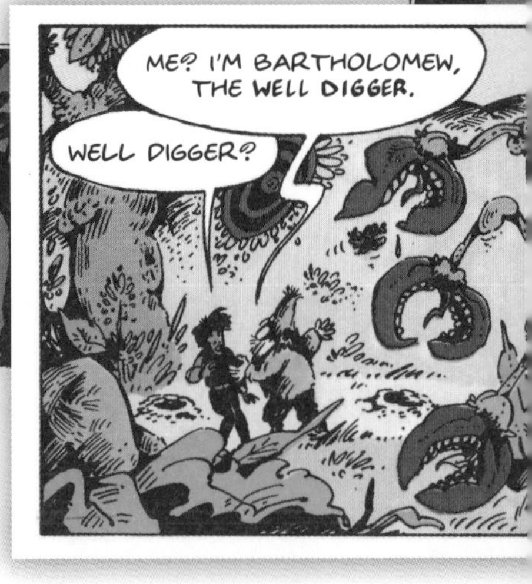
ME? I'M BARTHOLOMEW, THE **WELL DIGGER.**
WELL DIGGER?

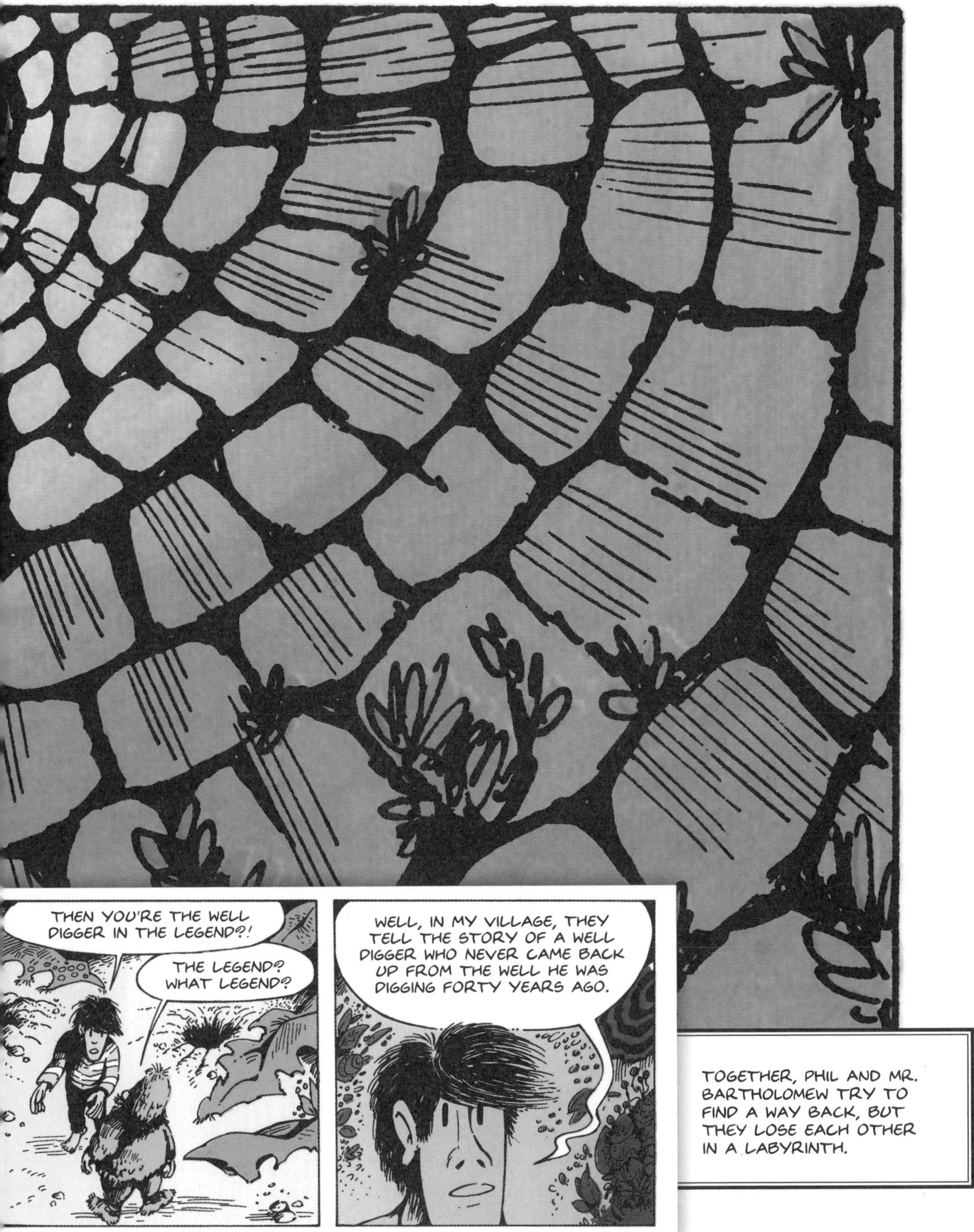
THEN YOU'RE THE WELL DIGGER IN THE LEGEND?!
THE LEGEND? WHAT LEGEND?
WELL, IN MY VILLAGE, THEY TELL THE STORY OF A WELL DIGGER WHO NEVER CAME BACK UP FROM THE WELL HE WAS DIGGING FORTY YEARS AGO.
TOGETHER, PHIL AND MR. BARTHOLOMEW TRY TO FIND A WAY BACK, BUT THEY LOSE EACH OTHER IN A LABYRINTH.

THE PHILEMON ADVENTURES

CAST AWAY ON THE LETTER A

THE WILD PIANO

THE SUSPENDED CASTLE

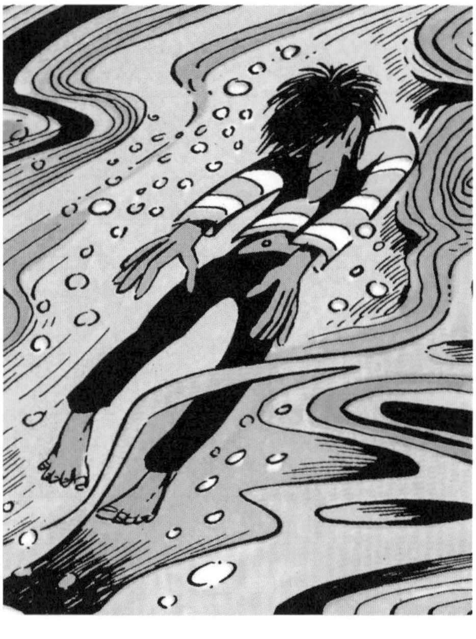

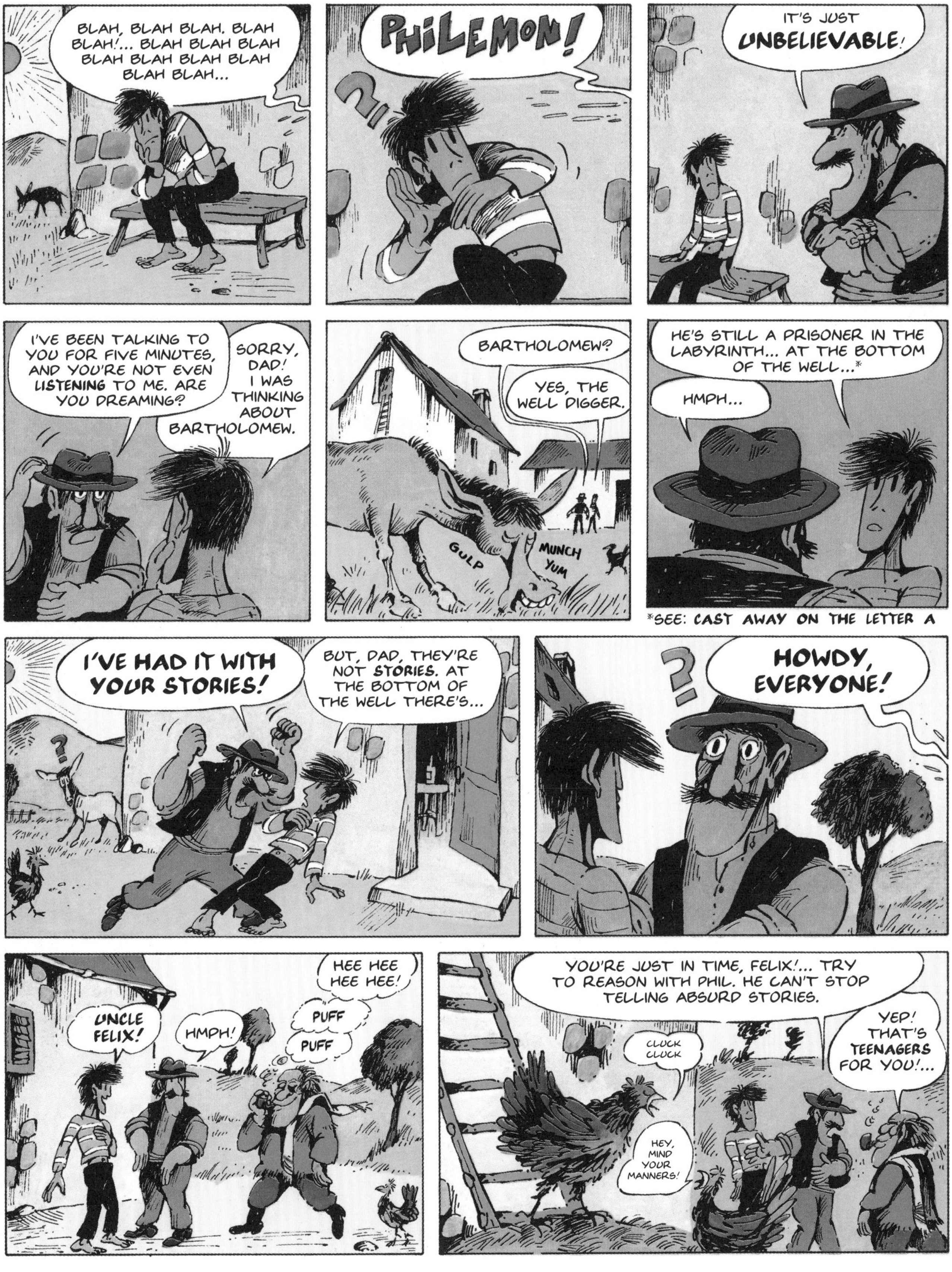
BLAH, BLAH BLAH. BLAH BLAH!... BLAH BLAH BLAH BLAH BLAH BLAH BLAH BLAH...
PHILEMON!
?
IT'S JUST UNBELIEVABLE!
I'VE BEEN TALKING TO YOU FOR FIVE MINUTES, AND YOU'RE NOT EVEN LISTENING TO ME. ARE YOU DREAMING?
SORRY, DAD! I WAS THINKING ABOUT BARTHOLOMEW.
BARTHOLOMEW?
YES, THE WELL DIGGER.
GULP
MUNCH YUM
HE'S STILL A PRISONER IN THE LABYRINTH... AT THE BOTTOM OF THE WELL...*
HMPH...
*SEE: CAST AWAY ON THE LETTER A
I'VE HAD IT WITH YOUR STORIES!
BUT, DAD, THEY'RE NOT STORIES. AT THE BOTTOM OF THE WELL THERE'S...
?
?
HOWDY, EVERYONE!
UNCLE FELIX!
HMPH!
HEE HEE HEE HEE!
PUFF
PUFF
YOU'RE JUST IN TIME, FELIX!... TRY TO REASON WITH PHIL. HE CAN'T STOP TELLING ABSURD STORIES.
CLUCK CLUCK
HEY, MIND YOUR MANNERS!
YEP! THAT'S TEENAGERS FOR YOU!...

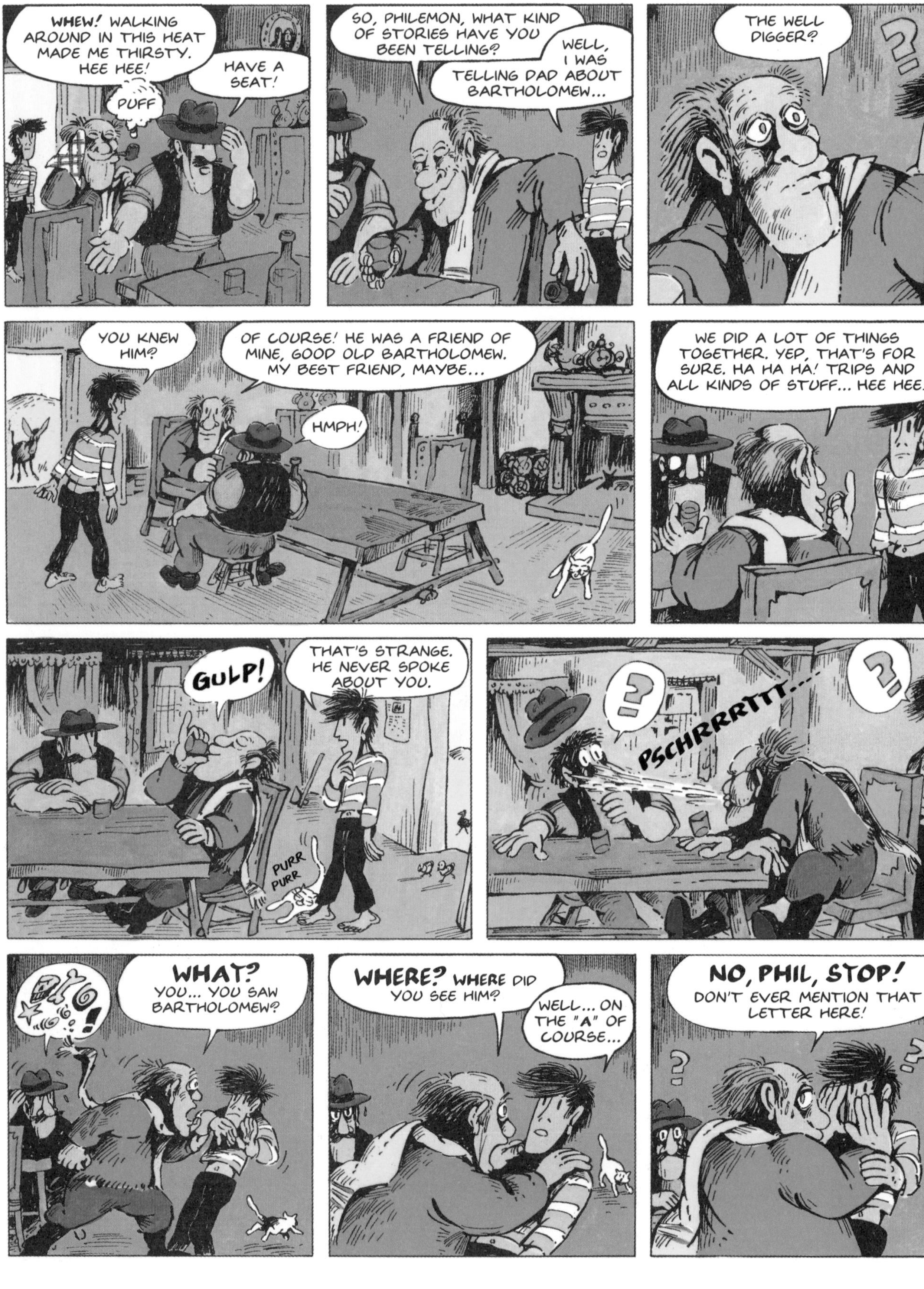
WHEW! WALKING AROUND IN THIS HEAT MADE ME THIRSTY. HEE HEE!
PUFF
HAVE A SEAT!
SO, PHILEMON, WHAT KIND OF STORIES HAVE YOU BEEN TELLING?
WELL, I WAS TELLING DAD ABOUT BARTHOLOMEW...
THE WELL DIGGER?
?
YOU KNEW HIM?
OF COURSE! HE WAS A FRIEND OF MINE, GOOD OLD BARTHOLOMEW. MY BEST FRIEND, MAYBE...
HMPH!
WE DID A LOT OF THINGS TOGETHER. YEP, THAT'S FOR SURE. HA HA HA! TRIPS AND ALL KINDS OF STUFF... HEE HEE!
GULP!
THAT'S STRANGE. HE NEVER SPOKE ABOUT YOU.
PURR PURR
?
PSCHRRRTTT...
?
WHAT? YOU... YOU SAW BARTHOLOMEW?
WHERE? WHERE DID YOU SEE HIM?
WELL... ON THE "A" OF COURSE...
NO, PHIL, STOP! DON'T EVER MENTION THAT LETTER HERE!
?
?

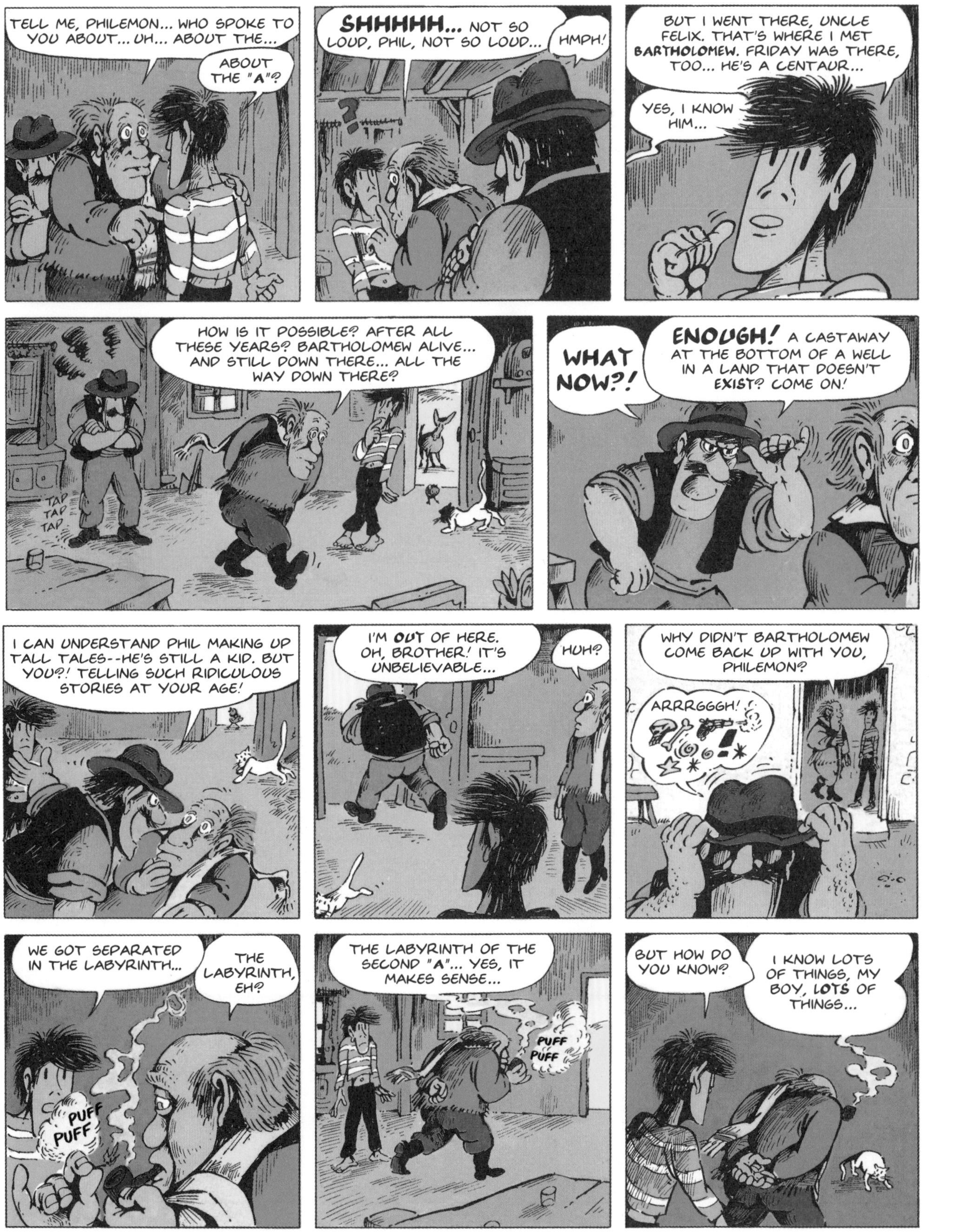
TELL ME, PHILEMON... WHO SPOKE TO YOU ABOUT... UH... ABOUT THE...
ABOUT THE "A"?
SHHHHH... NOT SO LOUD, PHIL, NOT SO LOUD...
HMPH!
BUT I WENT THERE, UNCLE FELIX. THAT'S WHERE I MET BARTHOLOMEW. FRIDAY WAS THERE, TOO... HE'S A CENTAUR...
YES, I KNOW HIM...
HOW IS IT POSSIBLE? AFTER ALL THESE YEARS? BARTHOLOMEW ALIVE... AND STILL DOWN THERE... ALL THE WAY DOWN THERE?
TAP TAP TAP
WHAT NOW?!
ENOUGH! A CASTAWAY AT THE BOTTOM OF A WELL IN A LAND THAT DOESN'T EXIST? COME ON!
I CAN UNDERSTAND PHIL MAKING UP TALL TALES--HE'S STILL A KID. BUT YOU?! TELLING SUCH RIDICULOUS STORIES AT YOUR AGE!
I'M OUT OF HERE. OH, BROTHER! IT'S UNBELIEVABLE...
HUH?
WHY DIDN'T BARTHOLOMEW COME BACK UP WITH YOU, PHILEMON?
ARRRGGGH!
WE GOT SEPARATED IN THE LABYRINTH...
THE LABYRINTH, EH?
PUFF PUFF
THE LABYRINTH OF THE SECOND "A"... YES, IT MAKES SENSE...
PUFF PUFF
BUT HOW DO YOU KNOW?
I KNOW LOTS OF THINGS, MY BOY, LOTS OF THINGS...

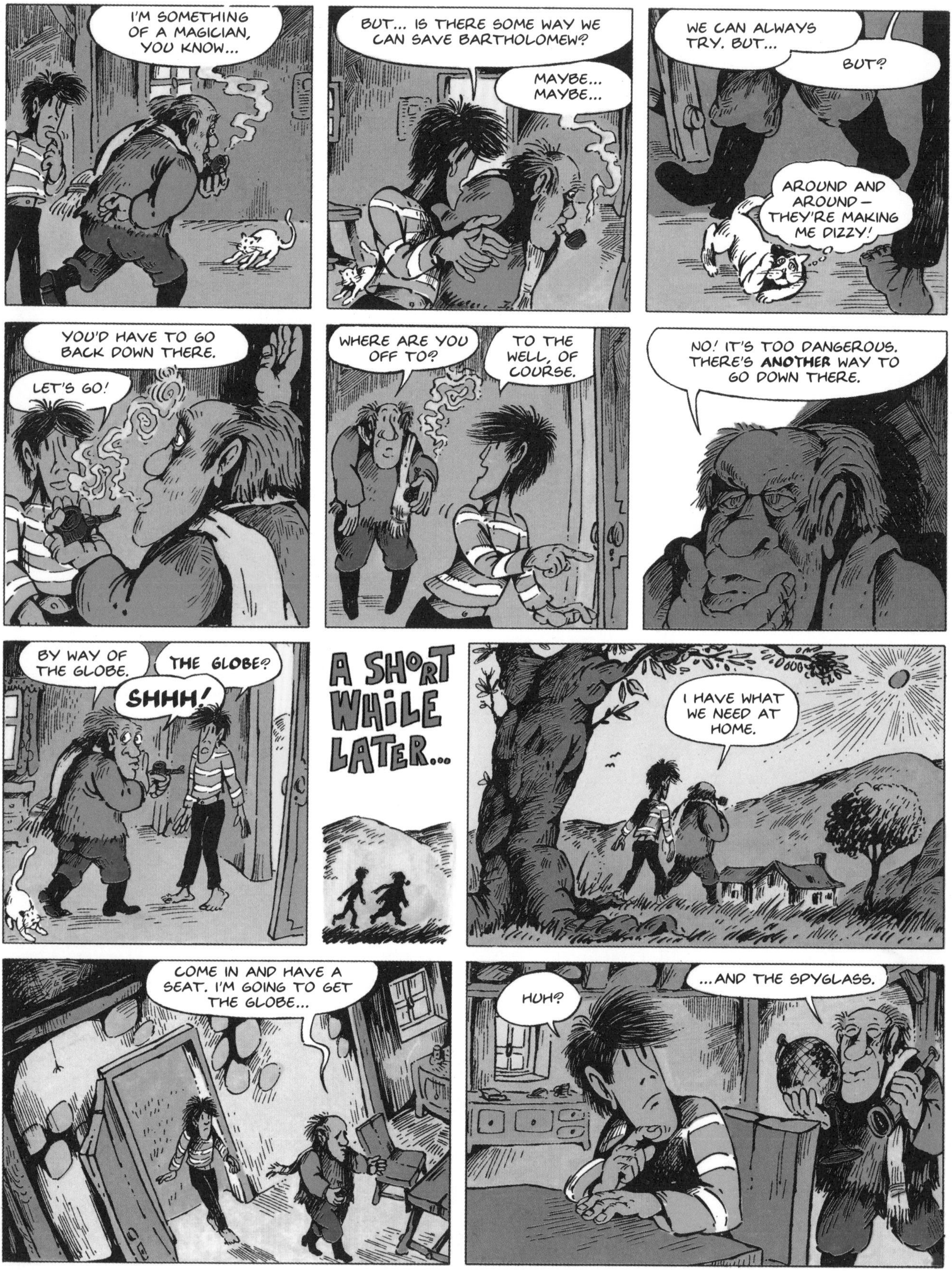
I'M SOMETHING OF A MAGICIAN, YOU KNOW...
BUT... IS THERE SOME WAY WE CAN SAVE BARTHOLOMEW?
MAYBE... MAYBE...
WE CAN ALWAYS TRY. BUT...
BUT?
AROUND AND AROUND — THEY'RE MAKING ME DIZZY!
YOU'D HAVE TO GO BACK DOWN THERE.
LET'S GO!
WHERE ARE YOU OFF TO?
TO THE WELL, OF COURSE.
NO! IT'S TOO DANGEROUS. THERE'S **ANOTHER** WAY TO GO DOWN THERE.
BY WAY OF THE GLOBE.
THE GLOBE?
SHHH!
A SHORT WHILE LATER...
I HAVE WHAT WE NEED AT HOME.
COME IN AND HAVE A SEAT. I'M GOING TO GET THE GLOBE...
HUH?
...AND THE SPYGLASS.

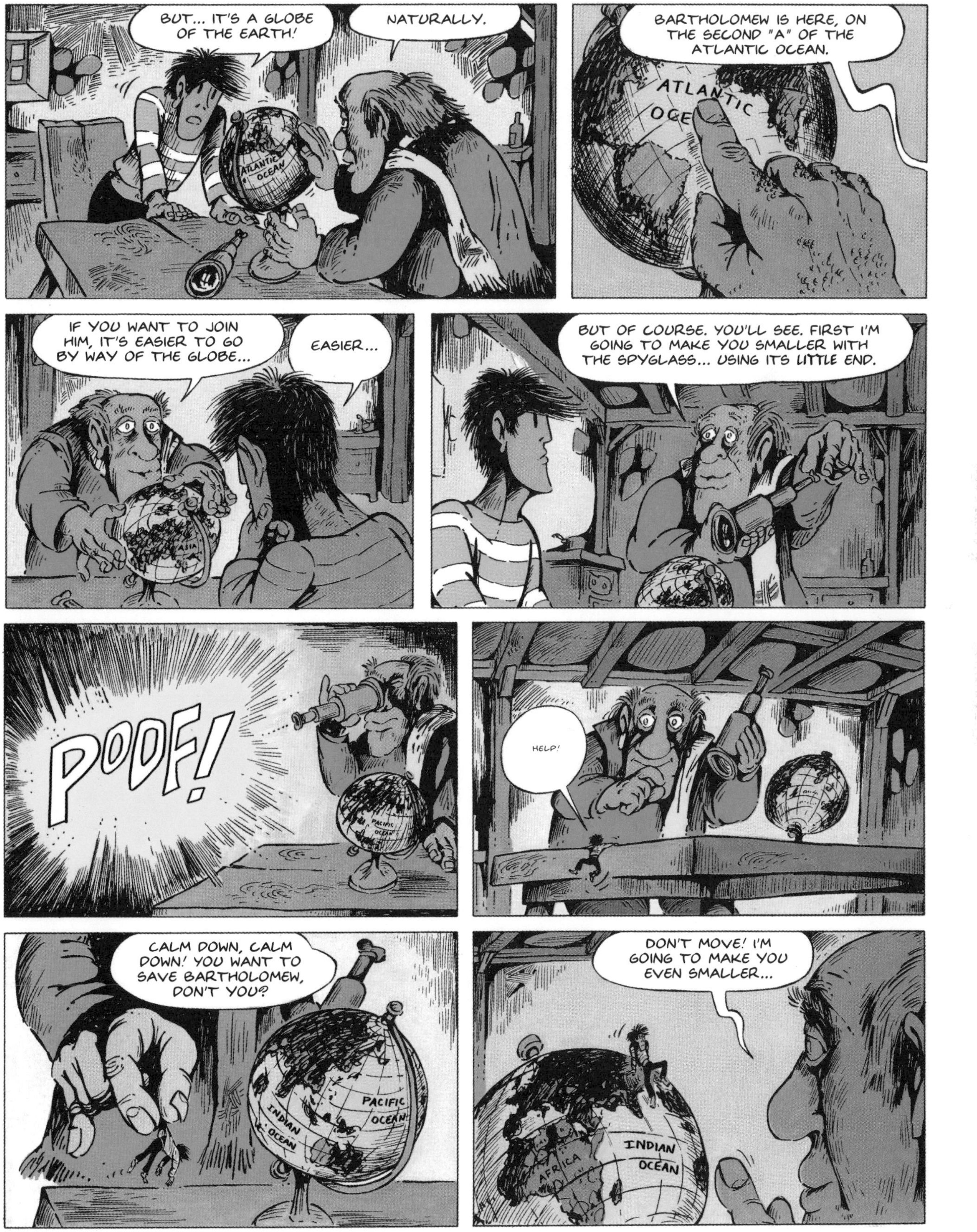
BUT... IT'S A GLOBE OF THE EARTH!
NATURALLY.
ATLANTIC OCEAN
BARTHOLOMEW IS HERE, ON THE SECOND "A" OF THE ATLANTIC OCEAN.
ATLANTIC OCE
IF YOU WANT TO JOIN HIM, IT'S EASIER TO GO BY WAY OF THE GLOBE...
EASIER...
ASIA
BUT OF COURSE. YOU'LL SEE. FIRST I'M GOING TO MAKE YOU SMALLER WITH THE SPYGLASS... USING ITS LITTLE END.
POOF!
PACIFIC OCEAN
HELP!
CALM DOWN, CALM DOWN! YOU WANT TO SAVE BARTHOLOMEW, DON'T YOU?
PACIFIC OCEAN
INDIAN OCEAN
DON'T MOVE! I'M GOING TO MAKE YOU EVEN SMALLER...
INDIAN OCEAN
AFRICA

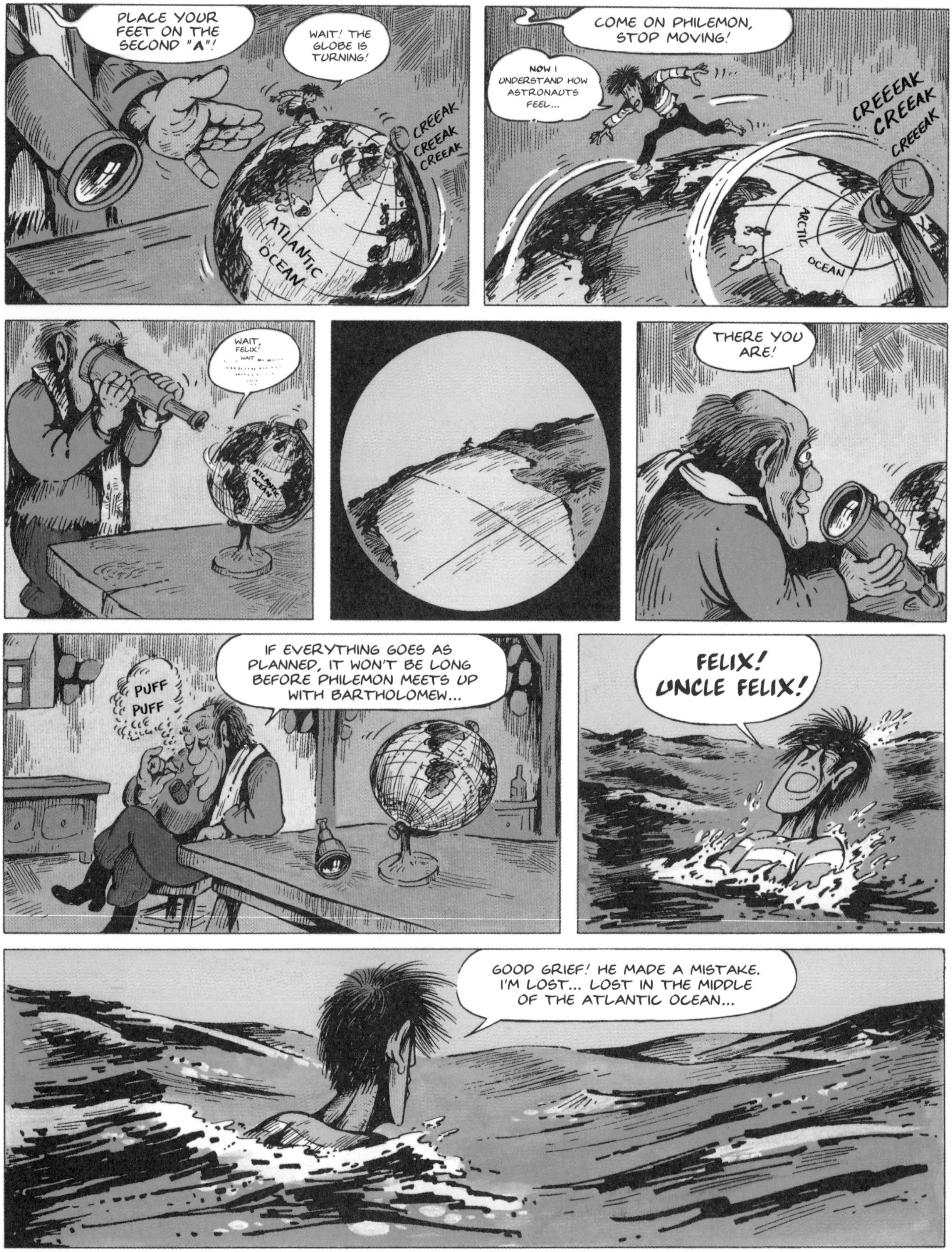
PLACE YOUR FEET ON THE SECOND "A"!
WAIT! THE GLOBE IS TURNING!
CREEAK CREEAK CREEAK
ATLANTIC OCEAN
COME ON PHILEMON, STOP MOVING!
NOW I UNDERSTAND HOW ASTRONAUTS FEEL...
CREEEAK CREEAK CREEEAK
ARCTIC OCEAN
WAIT, FELIX! WAIT
ATLANTIC OCEAN
THERE YOU ARE!
PUFF PUFF
IF EVERYTHING GOES AS PLANNED, IT WON'T BE LONG BEFORE PHILEMON MEETS UP WITH BARTHOLOMEW...
FELIX! UNCLE FELIX!
GOOD GRIEF! HE MADE A MISTAKE. I'M LOST... LOST IN THE MIDDLE OF THE ATLANTIC OCEAN...

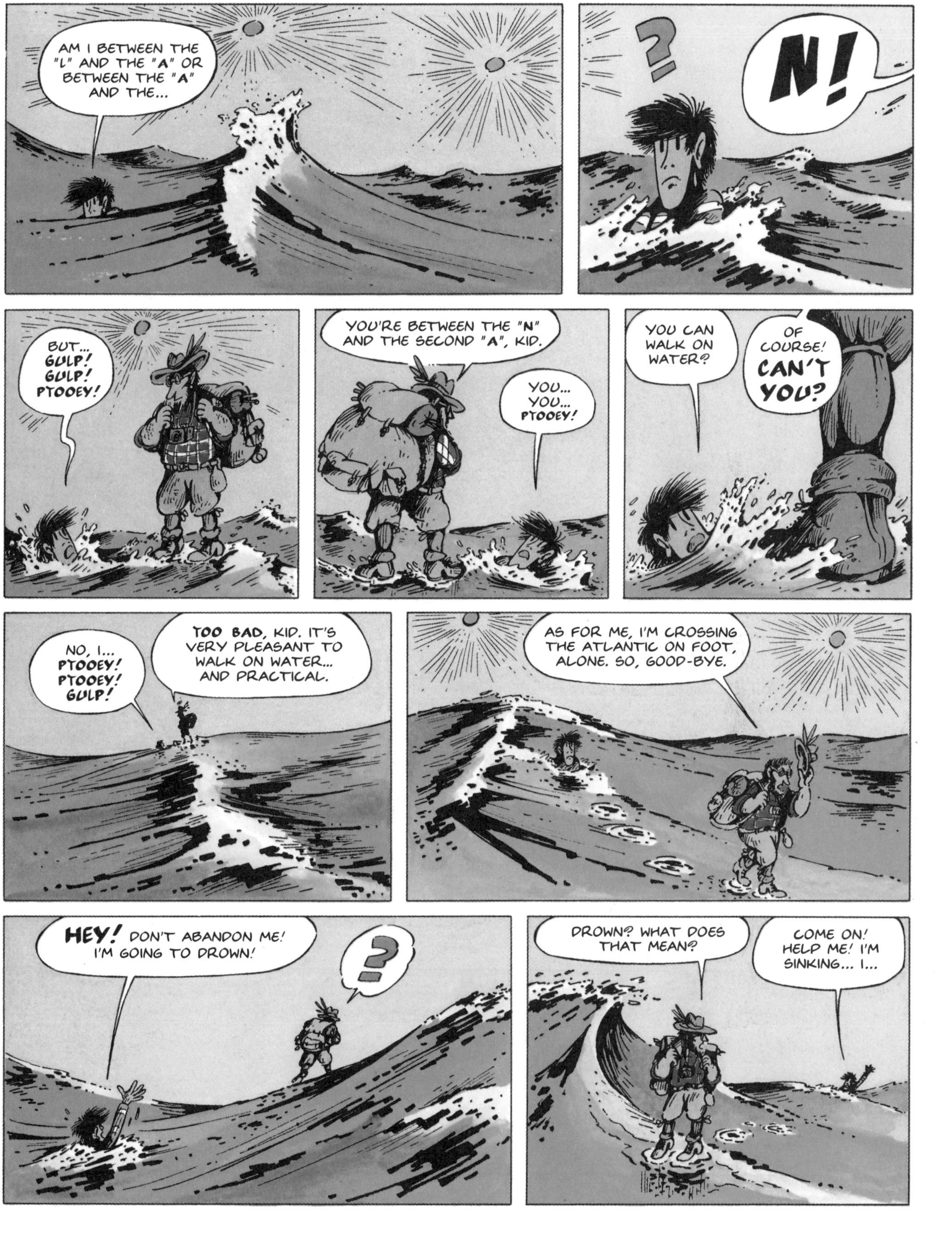
AM I BETWEEN THE "L" AND THE "A" OR BETWEEN THE "A" AND THE...
?
N!
BUT... GULP! GULP! PTOOEY!
YOU'RE BETWEEN THE "N" AND THE SECOND "A", KID.
YOU... YOU... PTOOEY!
YOU CAN WALK ON WATER?
OF COURSE! CAN'T YOU?
NO, I... PTOOEY! PTOOEY! GULP!
TOO BAD, KID. IT'S VERY PLEASANT TO WALK ON WATER... AND PRACTICAL.
AS FOR ME, I'M CROSSING THE ATLANTIC ON FOOT, ALONE. SO, GOOD-BYE.
HEY! DON'T ABANDON ME! I'M GOING TO DROWN!
?
DROWN? WHAT DOES THAT MEAN?
COME ON! HELP ME! I'M SINKING... I...

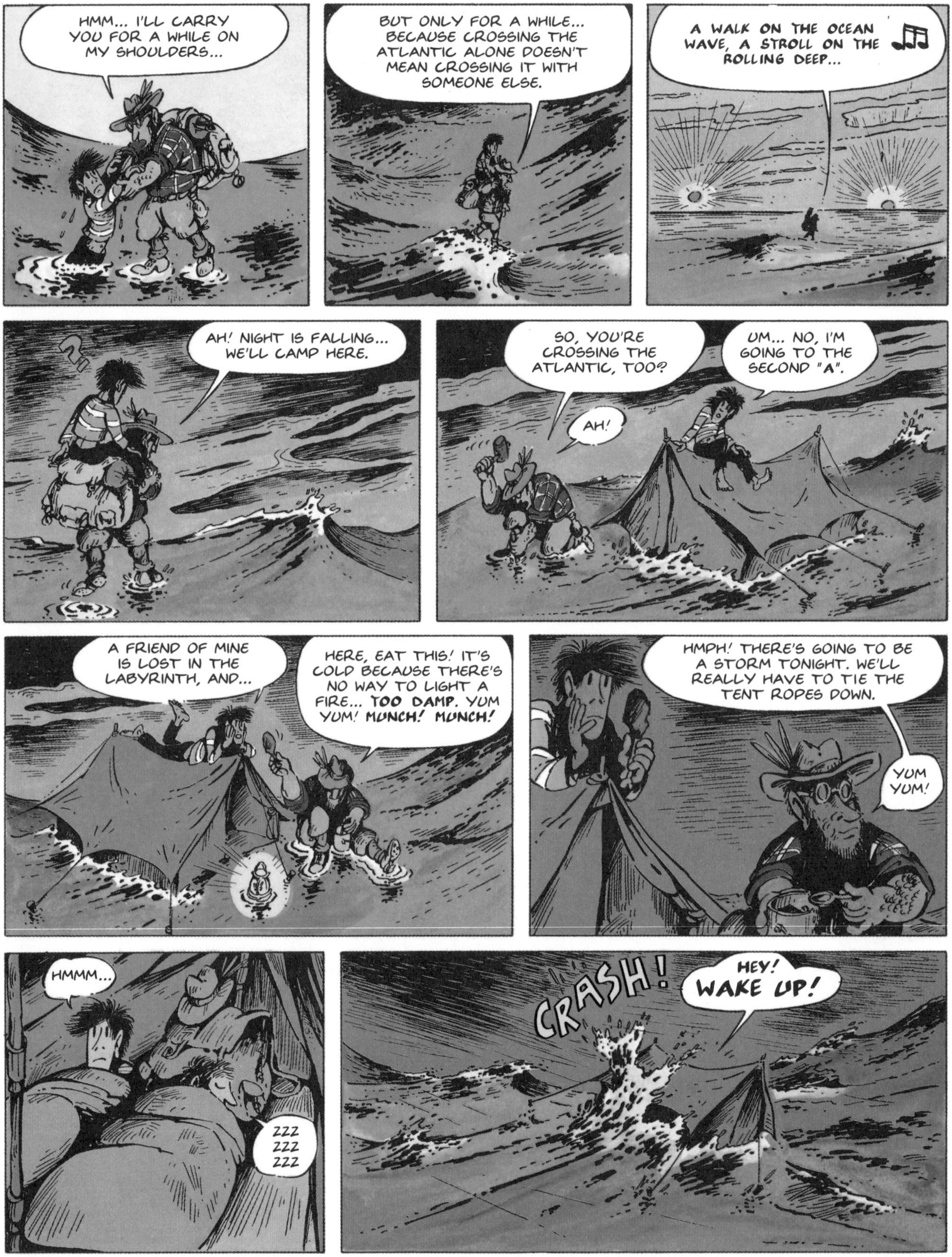
HMM... I'LL CARRY YOU FOR A WHILE ON MY SHOULDERS...
BUT ONLY FOR A WHILE... BECAUSE CROSSING THE ATLANTIC ALONE DOESN'T MEAN CROSSING IT WITH SOMEONE ELSE.
A WALK ON THE OCEAN WAVE, A STROLL ON THE ROLLING DEEP...
AH! NIGHT IS FALLING... WE'LL CAMP HERE.
SO, YOU'RE CROSSING THE ATLANTIC, TOO?
UM... NO, I'M GOING TO THE SECOND "A".
AH!
A FRIEND OF MINE IS LOST IN THE LABYRINTH, AND...
HERE, EAT THIS! IT'S COLD BECAUSE THERE'S NO WAY TO LIGHT A FIRE... TOO DAMP. YUM YUM! MUNCH! MUNCH!
HMPH! THERE'S GOING TO BE A STORM TONIGHT. WE'LL REALLY HAVE TO TIE THE TENT ROPES DOWN.
YUM YUM!
HMMM...
ZZZ ZZZ ZZZ
CRASH!
HEY! WAKE UP!

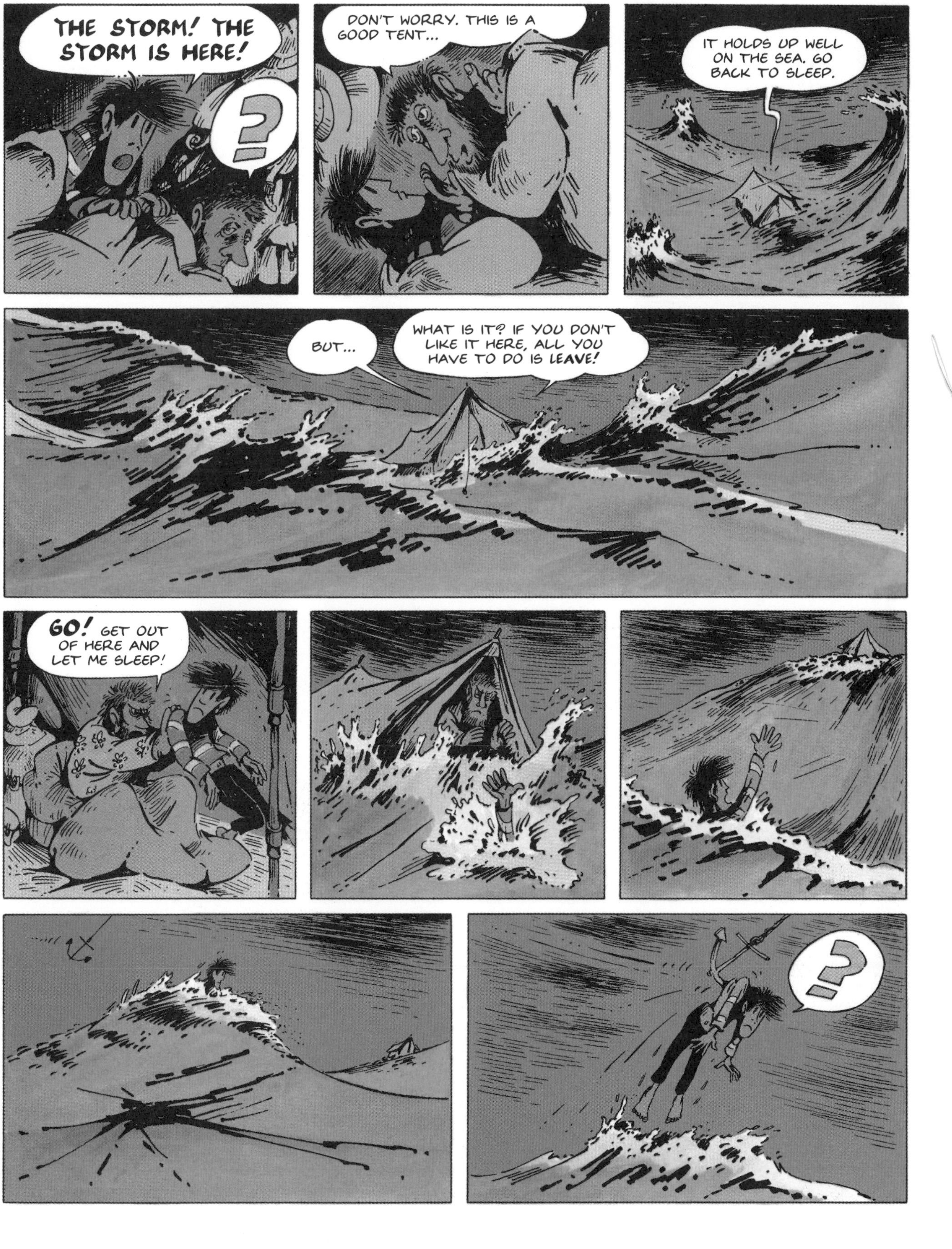
THE STORM! THE STORM IS HERE!
?
DON'T WORRY. THIS IS A GOOD TENT...
IT HOLDS UP WELL ON THE SEA. GO BACK TO SLEEP.
BUT...
WHAT IS IT? IF YOU DON'T LIKE IT HERE, ALL YOU HAVE TO DO IS LEAVE!
GO! GET OUT OF HERE AND LET ME SLEEP!
?

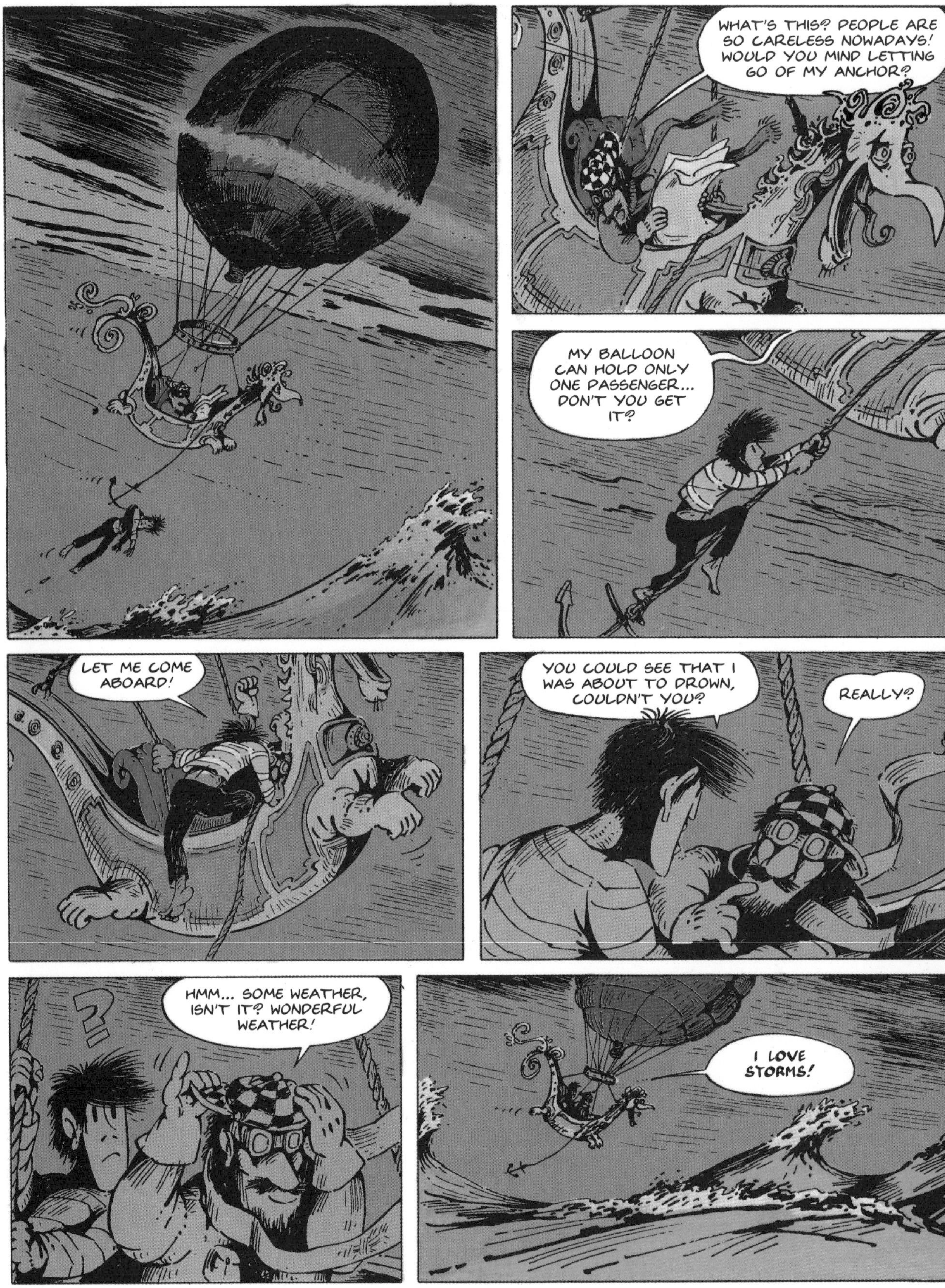
WHAT'S THIS? PEOPLE ARE SO CARELESS NOWADAYS! WOULD YOU MIND LETTING GO OF MY ANCHOR?
MY BALLOON CAN HOLD ONLY ONE PASSENGER... DON'T YOU GET IT?
LET ME COME ABOARD!
YOU COULD SEE THAT I WAS ABOUT TO DROWN, COULDN'T YOU?
REALLY?
?
HMM... SOME WEATHER, ISN'T IT? WONDERFUL WEATHER!
I LOVE STORMS!

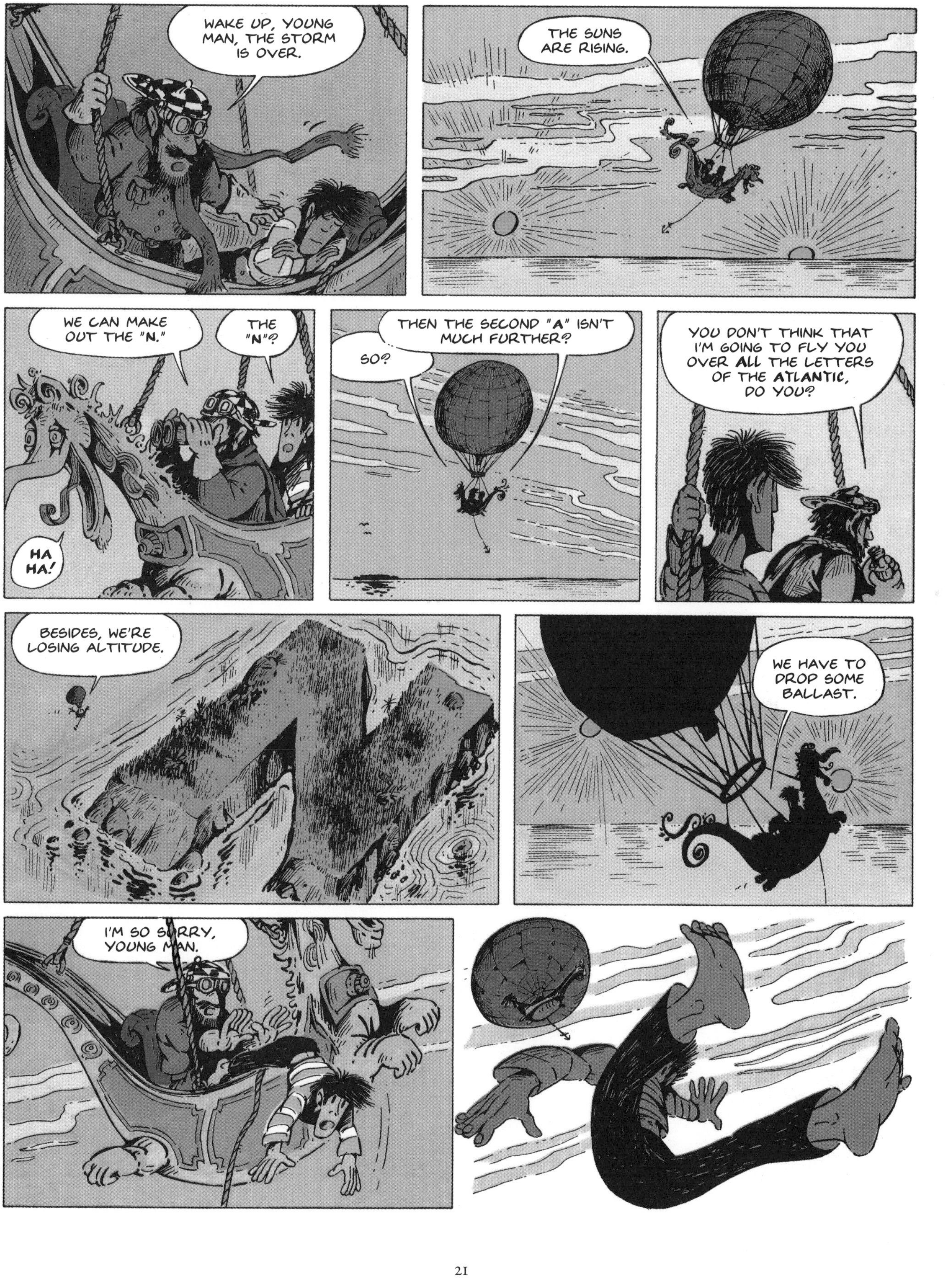
WAKE UP, YOUNG MAN, THE STORM IS OVER.
THE SUNS ARE RISING.
WE CAN MAKE OUT THE "N."
THE "N"?
HA HA!
SO?
THEN THE SECOND "A" ISN'T MUCH FURTHER?
YOU DON'T THINK THAT I'M GOING TO FLY YOU OVER ALL THE LETTERS OF THE ATLANTIC, DO YOU?
BESIDES, WE'RE LOSING ALTITUDE.
WE HAVE TO DROP SOME BALLAST.
I'M SO SORRY, YOUNG MAN.

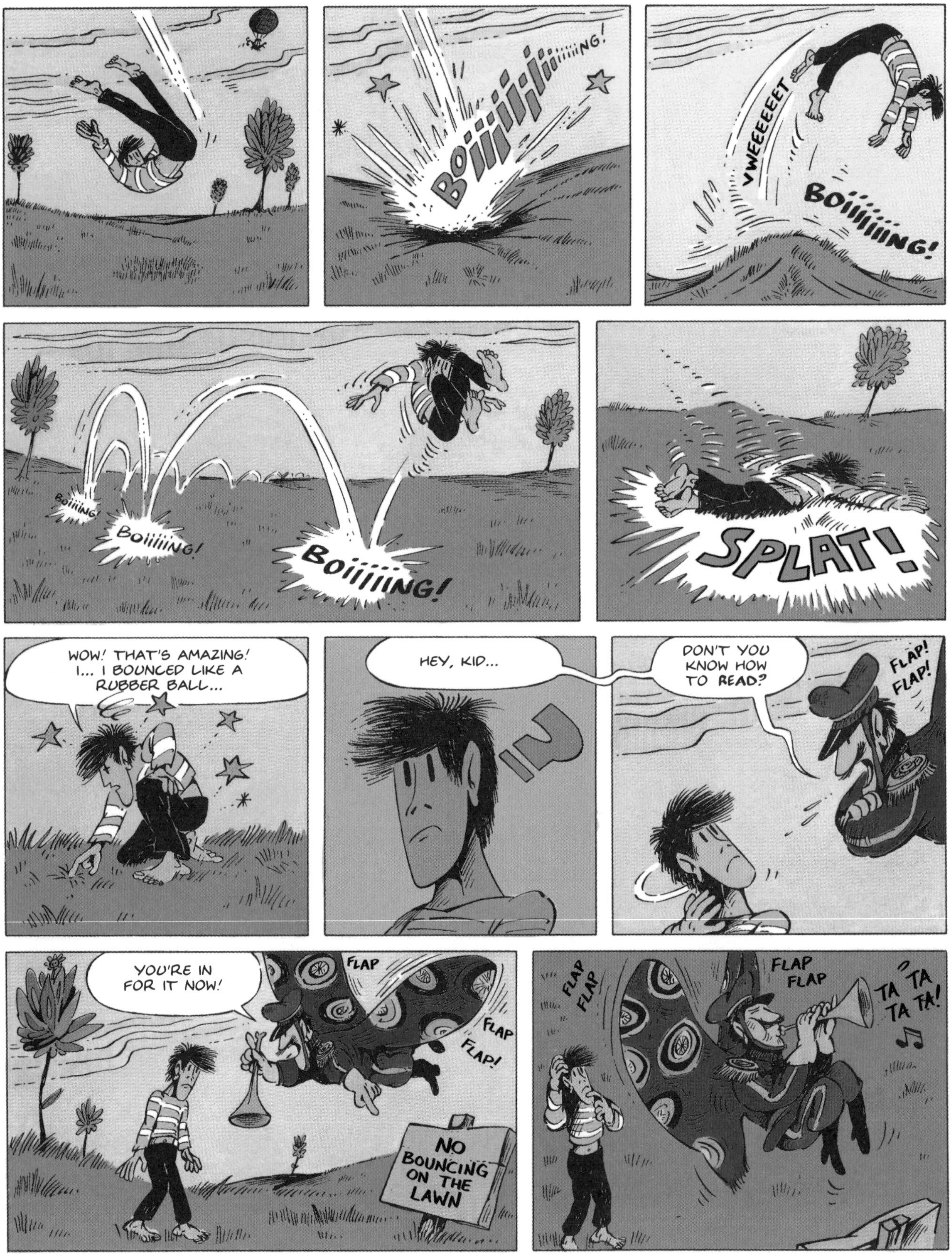
BOIIIIIIIIIIIIIING!
VWEEEEEET
BOIIIIIING!
BOIIING!
BOIIIING!
BOIIIIING!
SPLAT!
WOW! THAT'S AMAZING! I... I BOUNCED LIKE A RUBBER BALL...
HEY, KID...
DON'T YOU KNOW HOW TO READ?
FLAP! FLAP!
YOU'RE IN FOR IT NOW!
FLAP
FLAP
FLAP!
NO BOUNCING ON THE LAWN
FLAP FLAP
FLAP FLAP
TA TA TA TA!

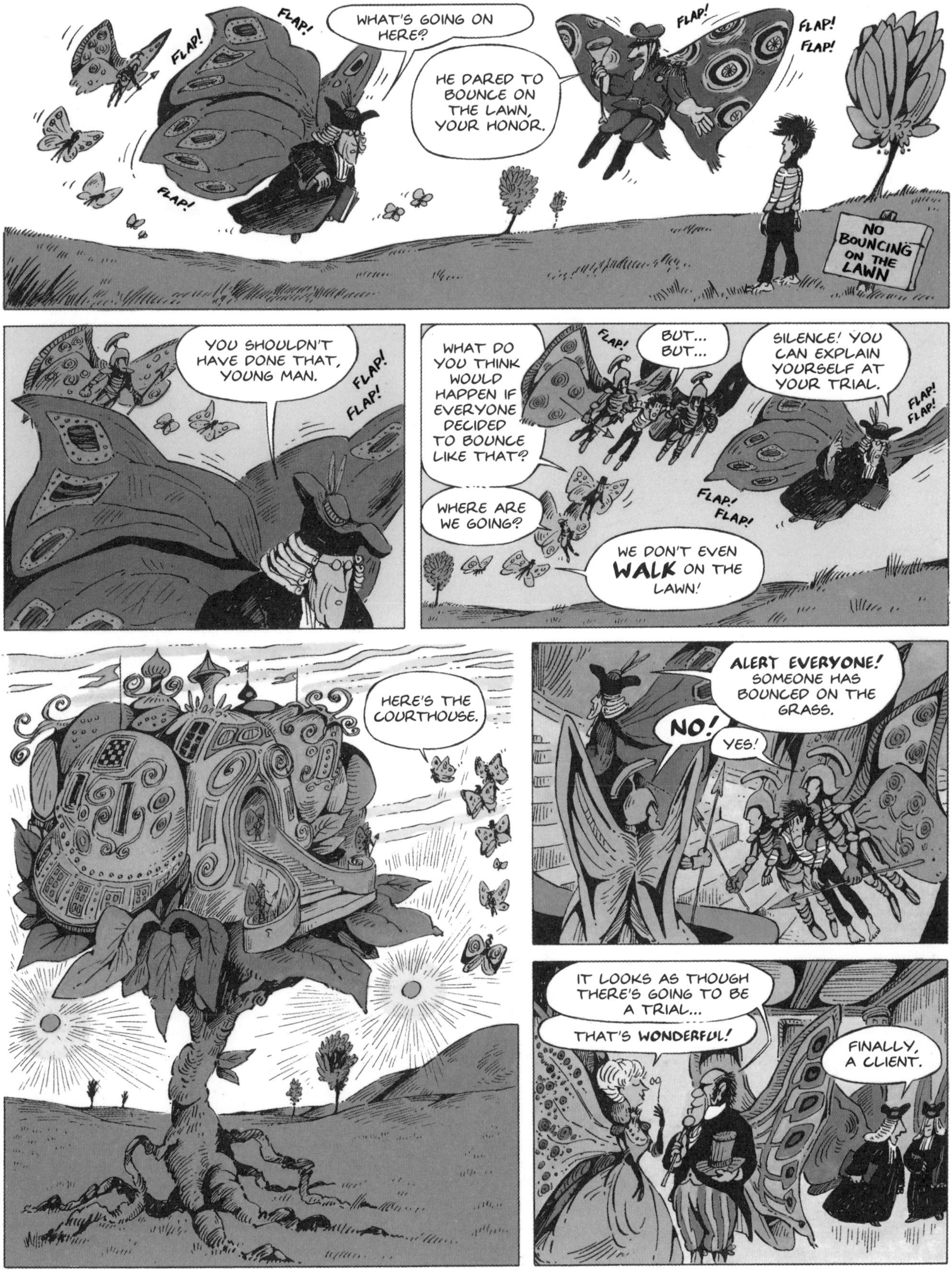
FLAP!
FLAP!
WHAT'S GOING ON HERE?
HE DARED TO BOUNCE ON THE LAWN, YOUR HONOR.
FLAP!
FLAP!
FLAP!
FLAP!
NO BOUNCING ON THE LAWN
YOU SHOULDN'T HAVE DONE THAT, YOUNG MAN.
FLAP!
FLAP!
WHAT DO YOU THINK WOULD HAPPEN IF EVERYONE DECIDED TO BOUNCE LIKE THAT?
FLAP!
BUT... BUT...
SILENCE! YOU CAN EXPLAIN YOURSELF AT YOUR TRIAL.
FLAP!
FLAP!
WHERE ARE WE GOING?
FLAP!
FLAP!
WE DON'T EVEN WALK ON THE LAWN!
HERE'S THE COURTHOUSE.
ALERT EVERYONE! SOMEONE HAS BOUNCED ON THE GRASS.
NO!
YES!
IT LOOKS AS THOUGH THERE'S GOING TO BE A TRIAL...
THAT'S WONDERFUL!
FINALLY, A CLIENT.

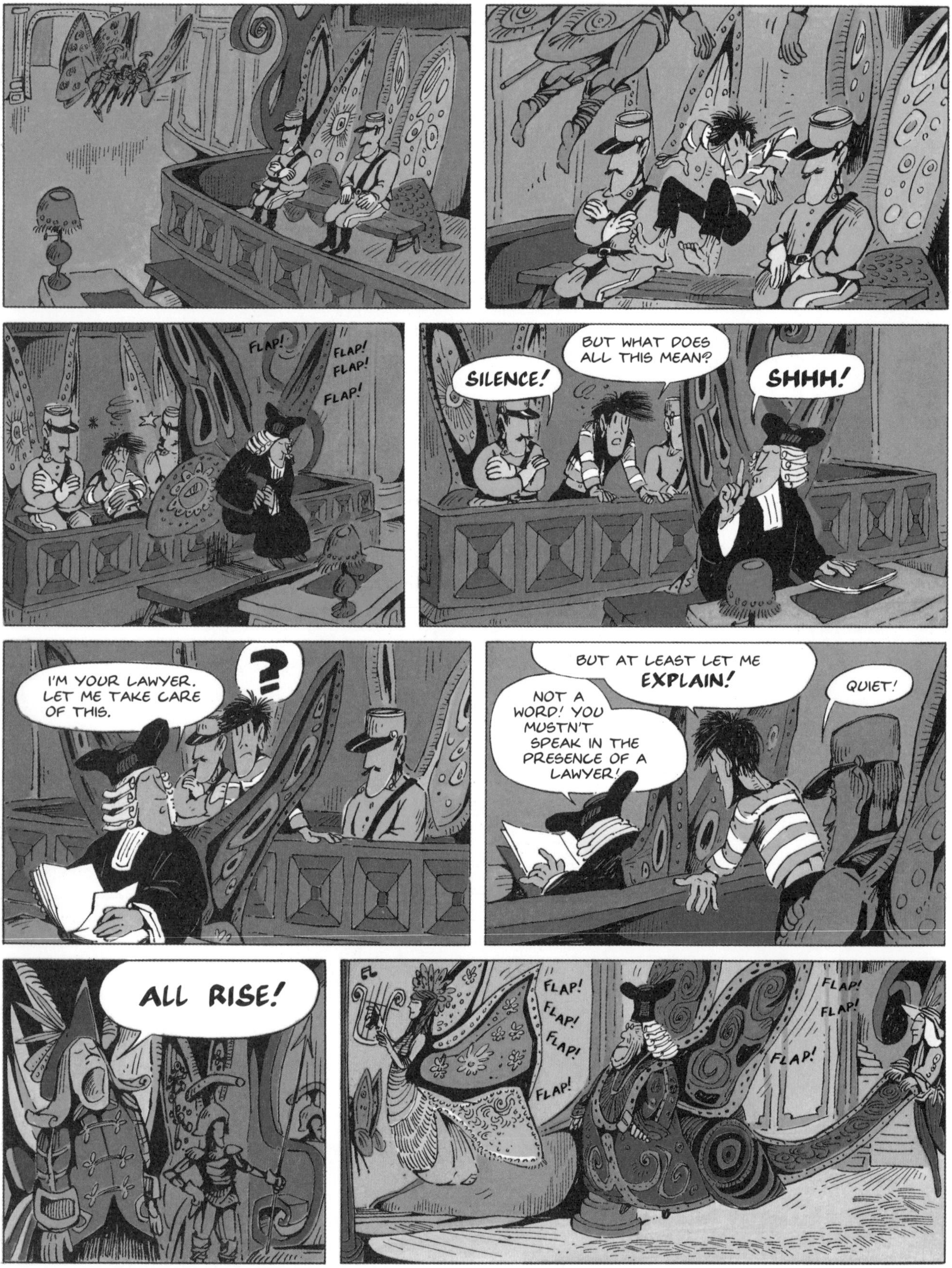
FLAP!
FLAP!
FLAP!
FLAP!
SILENCE!
BUT WHAT DOES ALL THIS MEAN?
SHHH!
I'M YOUR LAWYER. LET ME TAKE CARE OF THIS.
?
BUT AT LEAST LET ME EXPLAIN!
NOT A WORD! YOU MUSTN'T SPEAK IN THE PRESENCE OF A LAWYER!
QUIET!
ALL RISE!
FLAP!
FLAP!
FLAP!
FLAP!
FLAP!
FLAP!
FLAP!

Before the PHILEMON trial begins, we find it necessary to recount the history of the ban on bouncing on the lawn.

A very long time ago, the Grand Judge WZCHTZKPL AMPPTKPKL THE THIRD issued a decree forbidding the inhabitants of "N" from walking on the lawn. Since the entire island is covered with an immense lawn, the citizens were constantly breaking the law.

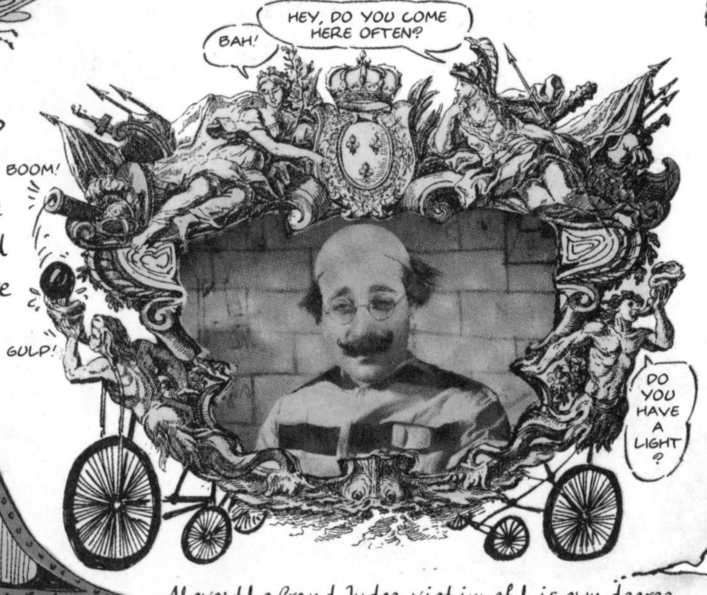

BAH!
HEY, DO YOU COME HERE OFTEN?
BOOM!
GULP!
DO YOU HAVE A LIGHT?

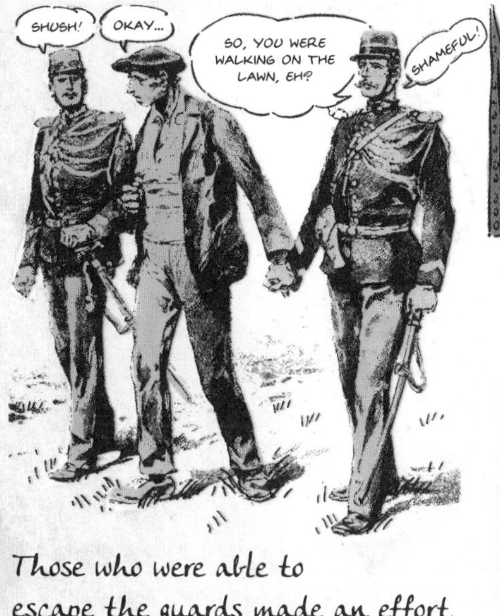

SHUSH!
OKAY...
SO, YOU WERE WALKING ON THE LAWN, EH?
SHAMEFUL!

Above: the Grand Judge, victim of his own decree.

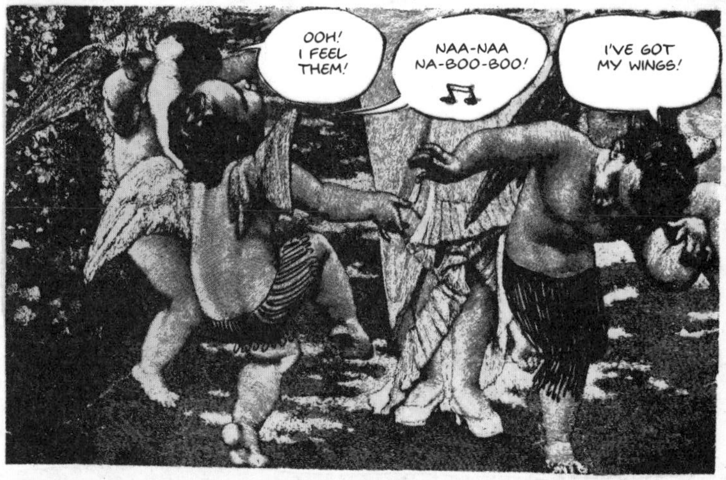

OOH! I FEEL THEM!
NAA-NAA NA-BOO-BOO!
I'VE GOT MY WINGS!

Those who were able to escape the guards made an effort to raise themselves above the lawn. From generation to generation, these efforts transformed the inhabitants – wings gradually began to appear on their backs, and it is thus that they began to fly. Thereafter, the decree was naturally changed into a ban on bouncing on the lawn.

Let's end this digression and continue with the trial.

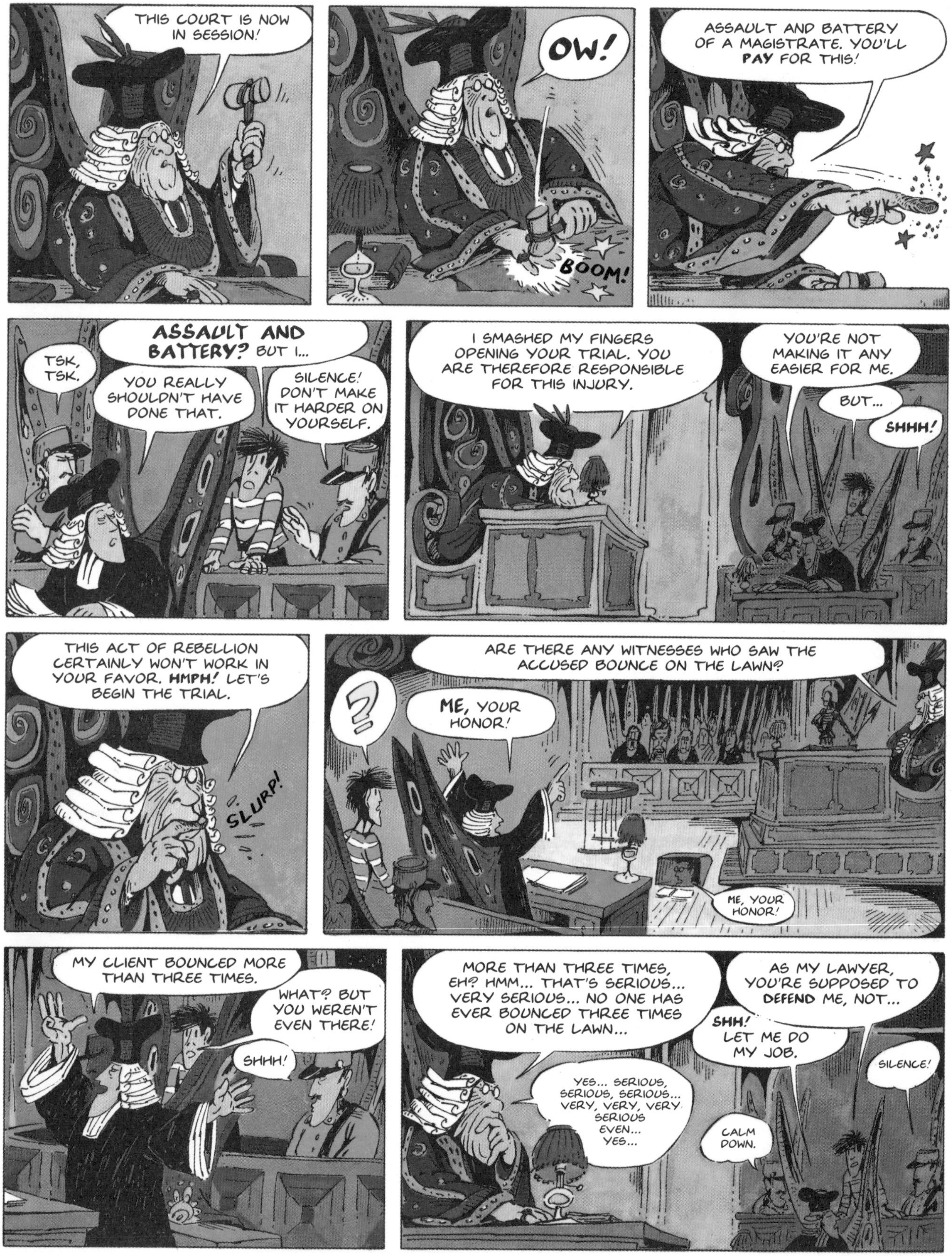
THIS COURT IS NOW IN SESSION!
OW!
BOOM!
ASSAULT AND BATTERY OF A MAGISTRATE. YOU'LL PAY FOR THIS!
ASSAULT AND BATTERY? BUT I...
TSK, TSK.
YOU REALLY SHOULDN'T HAVE DONE THAT.
SILENCE! DON'T MAKE IT HARDER ON YOURSELF.
I SMASHED MY FINGERS OPENING YOUR TRIAL. YOU ARE THEREFORE RESPONSIBLE FOR THIS INJURY.
YOU'RE NOT MAKING IT ANY EASIER FOR ME.
BUT...
SHHH!
THIS ACT OF REBELLION CERTAINLY WON'T WORK IN YOUR FAVOR. HMPH! LET'S BEGIN THE TRIAL.
SLURP!
ARE THERE ANY WITNESSES WHO SAW THE ACCUSED BOUNCE ON THE LAWN?
?
ME, YOUR HONOR!
ME, YOUR HONOR!
MY CLIENT BOUNCED MORE THAN THREE TIMES.
WHAT? BUT YOU WEREN'T EVEN THERE!
SHHH!
MORE THAN THREE TIMES, EH? HMM... THAT'S SERIOUS... VERY SERIOUS... NO ONE HAS EVER BOUNCED THREE TIMES ON THE LAWN...
YES... SERIOUS, SERIOUS, SERIOUS... VERY, VERY, VERY SERIOUS EVEN... YES...
AS MY LAWYER, YOU'RE SUPPOSED TO DEFEND ME, NOT...
SHH! LET ME DO MY JOB.
CALM DOWN.
SILENCE!

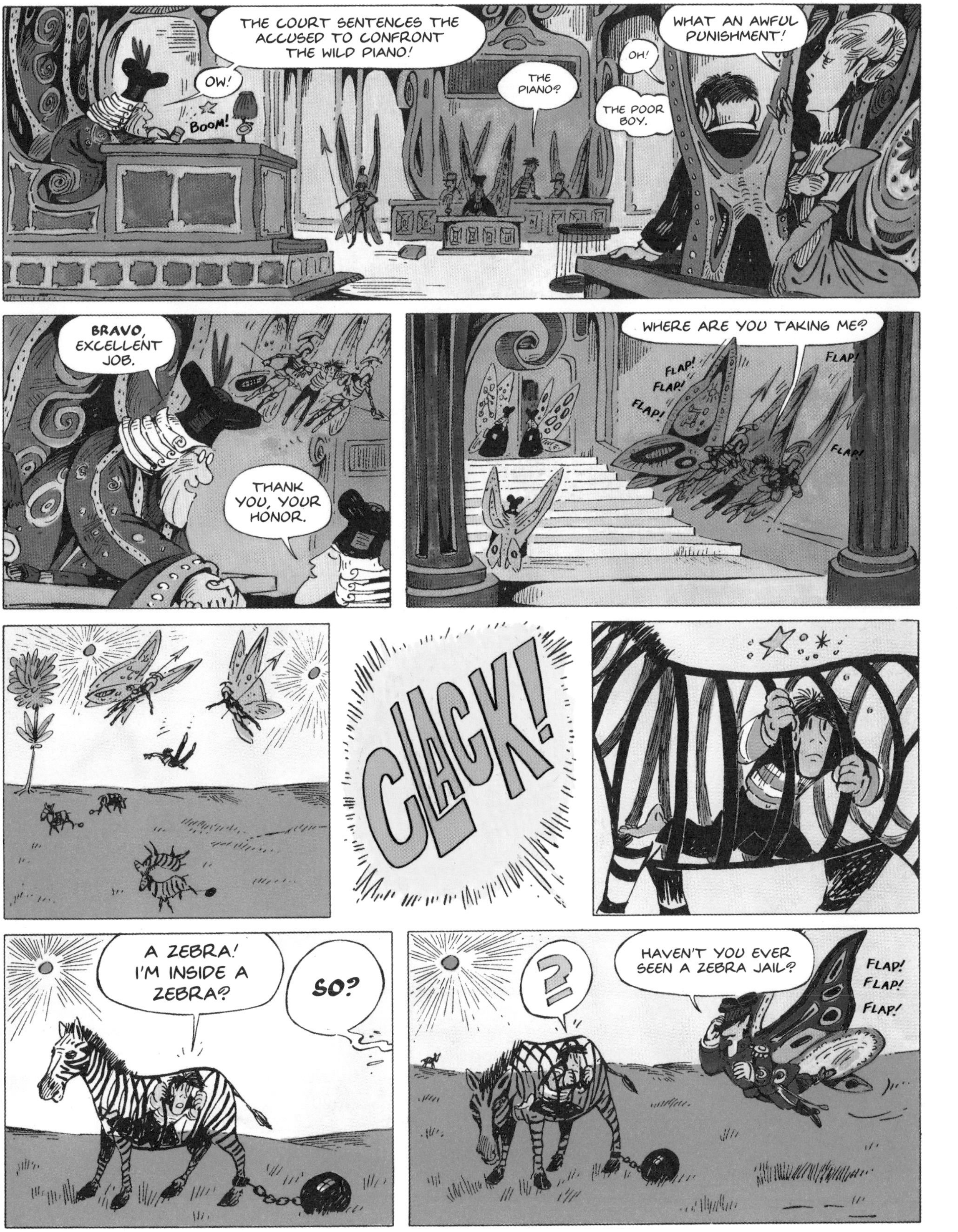
THE COURT SENTENCES THE ACCUSED TO CONFRONT THE WILD PIANO!
OW!
BOOM!
THE PIANO?
OH!
THE POOR BOY.
WHAT AN AWFUL PUNISHMENT!
BRAVO, EXCELLENT JOB.
THANK YOU, YOUR HONOR.
WHERE ARE YOU TAKING ME?
FLAP!
FLAP!
FLAP!
FLAP!
FLAP!
CLACK!
A ZEBRA! I'M INSIDE A ZEBRA?
SO?
?
HAVEN'T YOU EVER SEEN A ZEBRA JAIL?
FLAP!
FLAP!
FLAP!

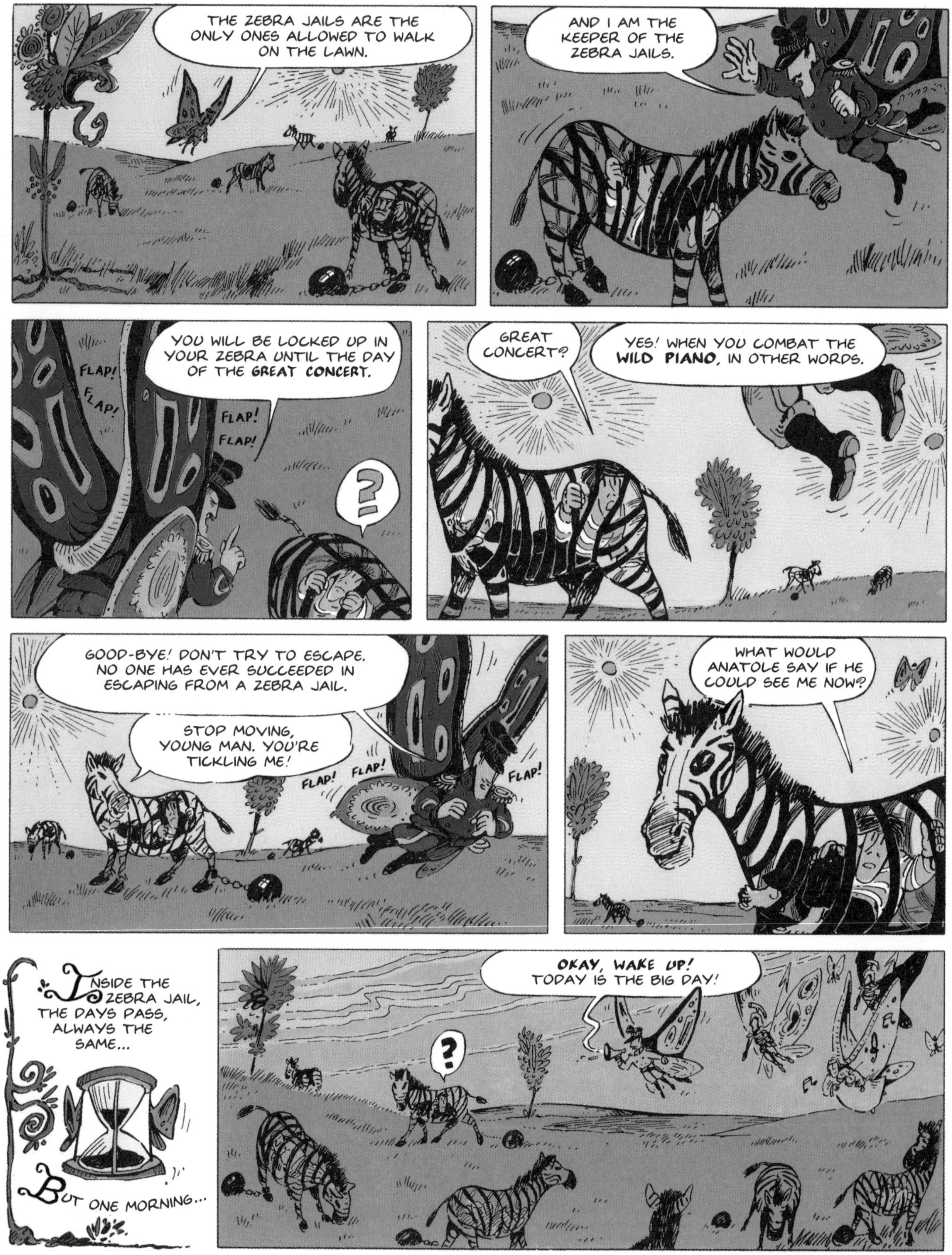
THE ZEBRA JAILS ARE THE ONLY ONES ALLOWED TO WALK ON THE LAWN.
AND I AM THE KEEPER OF THE ZEBRA JAILS.
FLAP! FLAP!
YOU WILL BE LOCKED UP IN YOUR ZEBRA UNTIL THE DAY OF THE GREAT CONCERT.
FLAP! FLAP!
?
GREAT CONCERT?
YES! WHEN YOU COMBAT THE WILD PIANO, IN OTHER WORDS.
GOOD-BYE! DON'T TRY TO ESCAPE. NO ONE HAS EVER SUCCEEDED IN ESCAPING FROM A ZEBRA JAIL.
STOP MOVING, YOUNG MAN. YOU'RE TICKLING ME!
FLAP! FLAP! FLAP!
WHAT WOULD ANATOLE SAY IF HE COULD SEE ME NOW?
INSIDE THE ZEBRA JAIL, THE DAYS PASS, ALWAYS THE SAME...
BUT ONE MORNING...
OKAY, WAKE UP! TODAY IS THE BIG DAY!
?

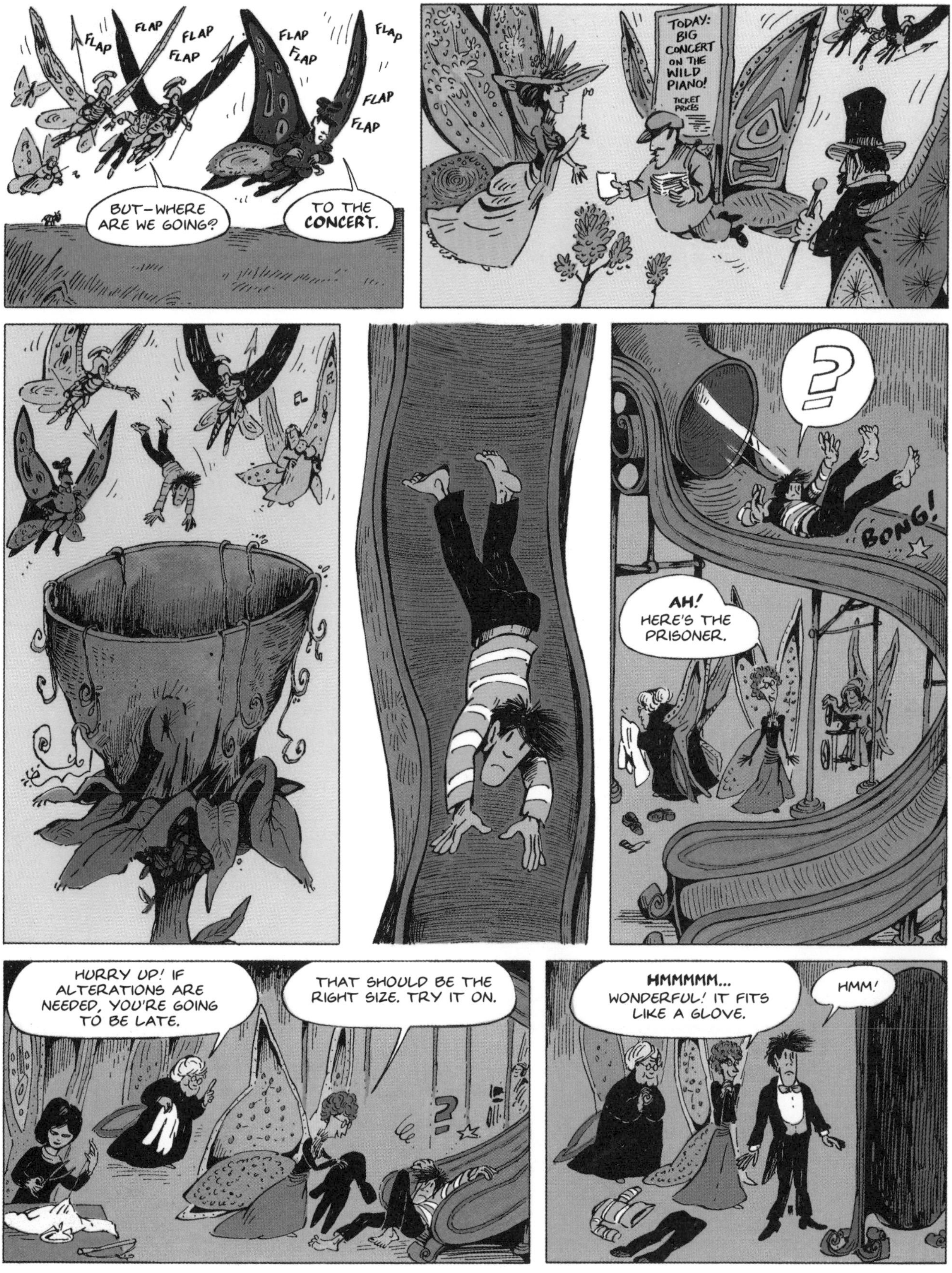

FLAP
FLAP
FLAP
FLAP
FLAP
FLAP
FLAP
FLAP
FLAP
BUT—WHERE ARE WE GOING?
TO THE CONCERT.
TODAY: BIG CONCERT ON THE WILD PIANO!
TICKET PRICES
?
BONG!
AH! HERE'S THE PRISONER.
HURRY UP! IF ALTERATIONS ARE NEEDED, YOU'RE GOING TO BE LATE.
THAT SHOULD BE THE RIGHT SIZE. TRY IT ON.
?
HMMMMM... WONDERFUL! IT FITS LIKE A GLOVE.
HMM!

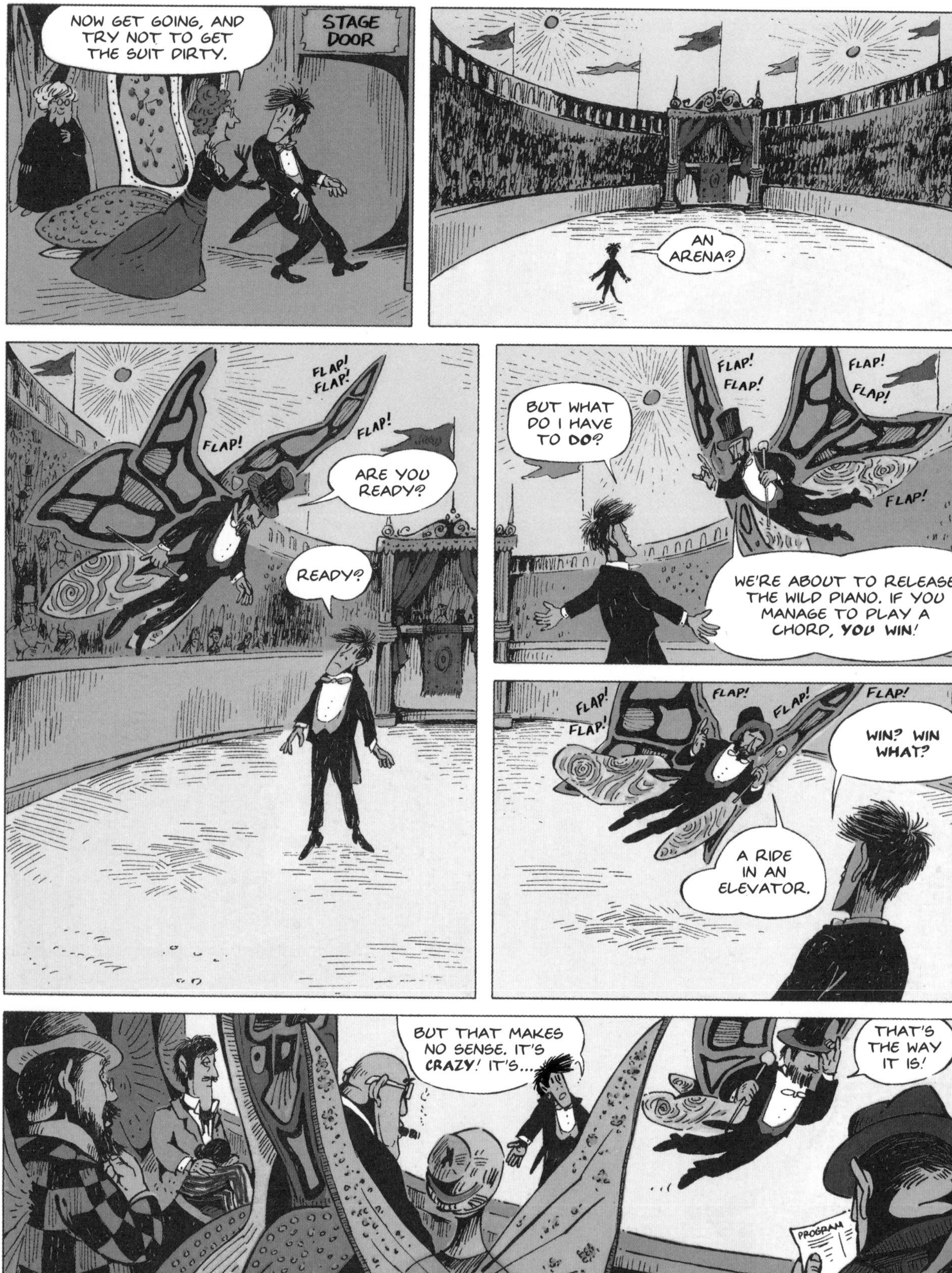
NOW GET GOING, AND TRY NOT TO GET THE SUIT DIRTY.
STAGE DOOR
AN ARENA?
FLAP! FLAP!
FLAP!
FLAP!
ARE YOU READY?
READY?
BUT WHAT DO I HAVE TO **DO**?
FLAP!
FLAP!
FLAP!
FLAP!
FLAP!
WE'RE ABOUT TO RELEASE THE WILD PIANO. IF YOU MANAGE TO PLAY A CHORD, **YOU WIN**!
FLAP!
FLAP!
FLAP!
FLAP!
FLAP!
WIN? WIN WHAT?
A RIDE IN AN ELEVATOR.
BUT THAT MAKES NO SENSE. IT'S ***CRAZY***! IT'S...
THAT'S THE WAY IT IS!
PROGRAM

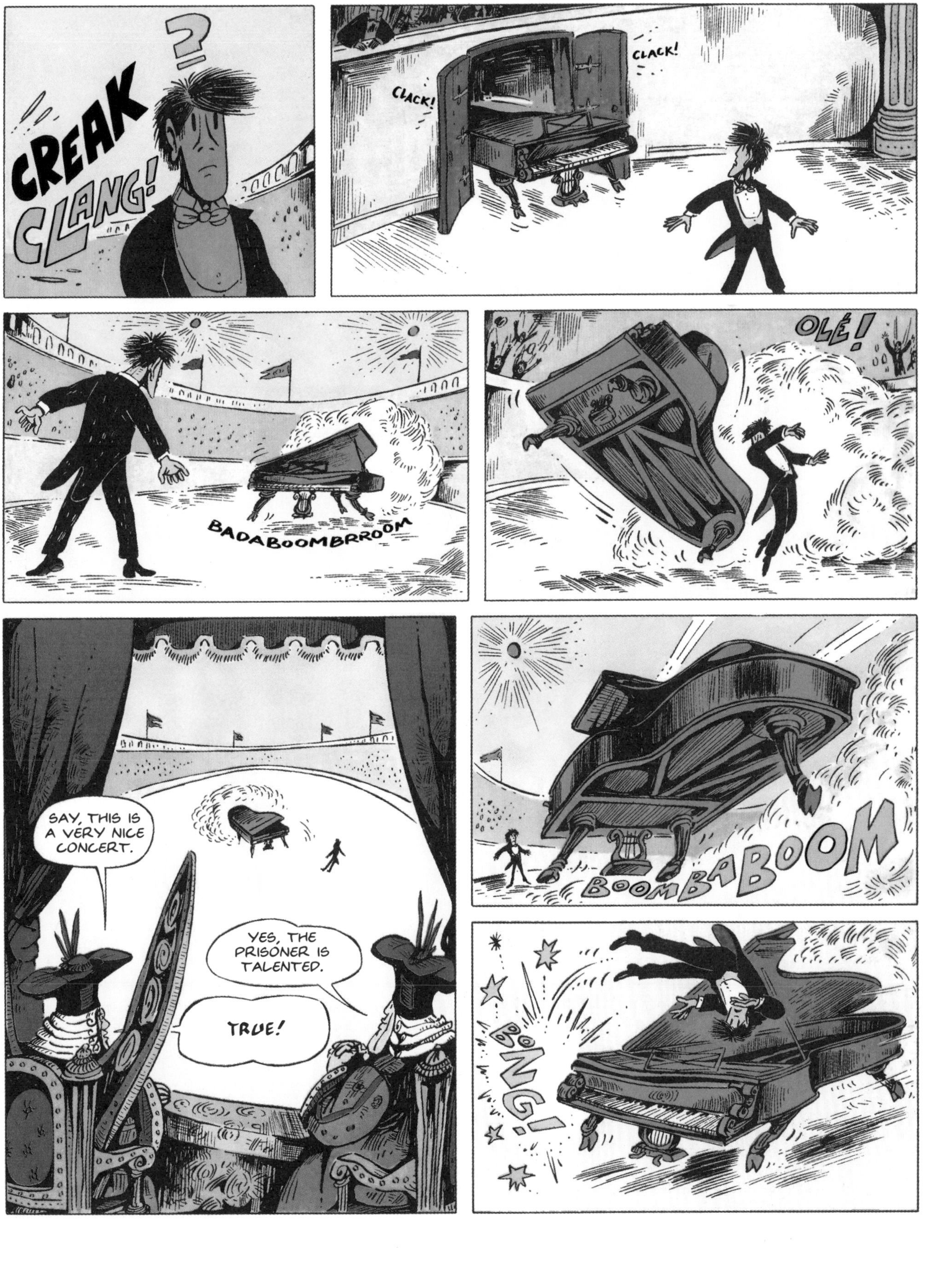
?
CREAK
CLANG!
CLACK!
CLACK!
BADABOOMBRROOM
OLÉ!
BOOMBABOOM
SAY, THIS IS A VERY NICE CONCERT.
YES, THE PRISONER IS TALENTED.
TRUE!
BONG!

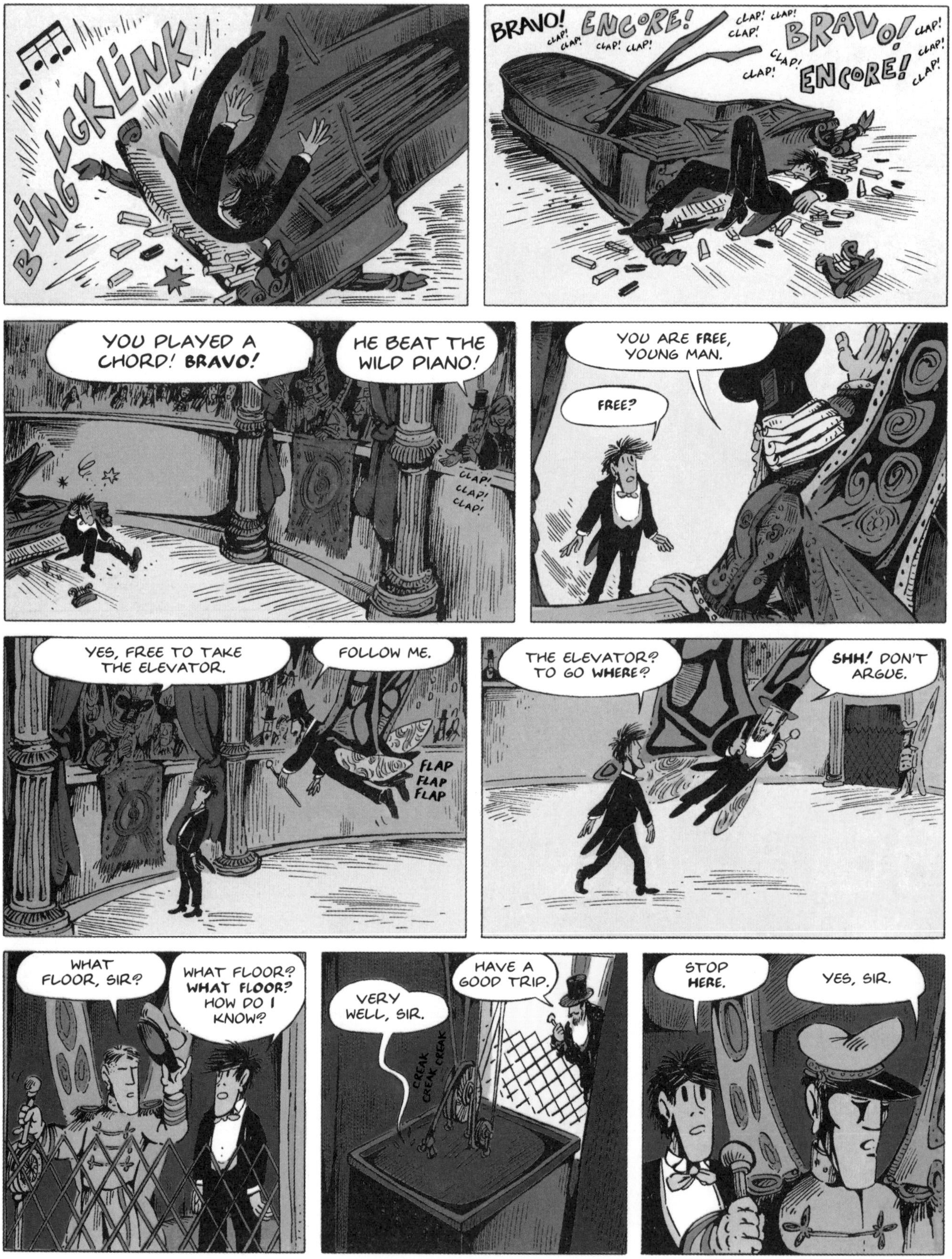
BLINGLGKLINK
BRAVO!
CLAP! CLAP!
ENCORE!
CLAP! CLAP!
CLAP! CLAP! CLAP! CLAP!
BRAVO!
CLAP! CLAP! CLAP!
ENCORE!
CLAP! CLAP! CLAP!
YOU PLAYED A CHORD! BRAVO!
HE BEAT THE WILD PIANO!
CLAP! CLAP! CLAP!
YOU ARE FREE, YOUNG MAN.
FREE?
YES, FREE TO TAKE THE ELEVATOR.
FOLLOW ME.
FLAP FLAP FLAP
THE ELEVATOR? TO GO WHERE?
SHH! DON'T ARGUE.
WHAT FLOOR, SIR?
WHAT FLOOR? WHAT FLOOR? HOW DO I KNOW?
VERY WELL, SIR.
HAVE A GOOD TRIP.
CREAK CREAK CREAK
STOP HERE.
YES, SIR.

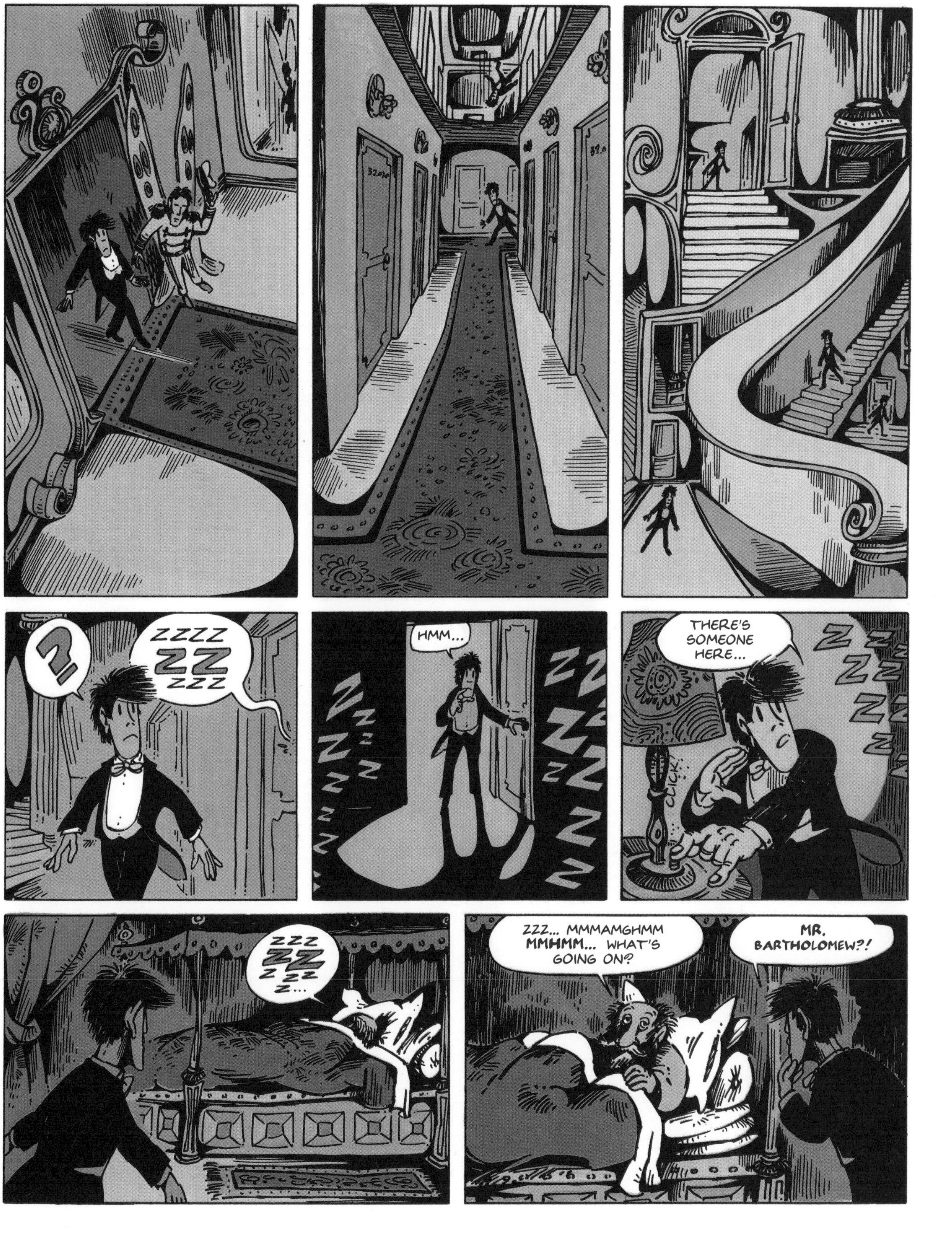

?!
ZZZZ ZZ ZZZ
HMM...
Z Z Z Z
THERE'S SOMEONE HERE...
CLICK
ZZZ ZZ ZZZ Z...
ZZZ... MMMAMGHMM MMHMM... WHAT'S GOING ON?
MR. BARTHOLOMEW?!

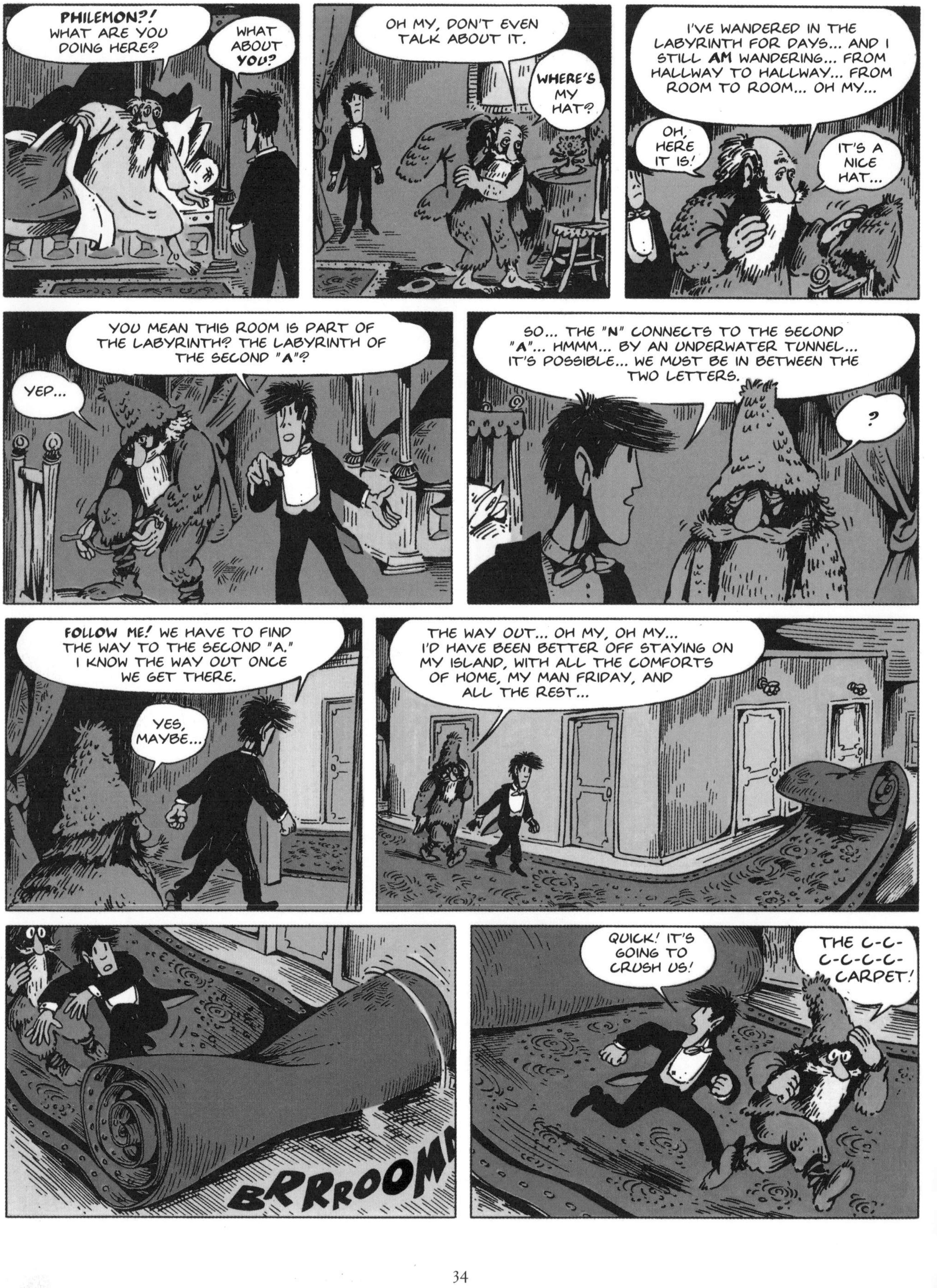
PHILEMON?! WHAT ARE YOU DOING HERE?
WHAT ABOUT YOU?
OH MY, DON'T EVEN TALK ABOUT IT.
WHERE'S MY HAT?
I'VE WANDERED IN THE LABYRINTH FOR DAYS... AND I STILL AM WANDERING... FROM HALLWAY TO HALLWAY... FROM ROOM TO ROOM... OH MY...
OH, HERE IT IS!
IT'S A NICE HAT...
YOU MEAN THIS ROOM IS PART OF THE LABYRINTH? THE LABYRINTH OF THE SECOND "A"?
YEP...
SO... THE "N" CONNECTS TO THE SECOND "A"... HMMM... BY AN UNDERWATER TUNNEL... IT'S POSSIBLE... WE MUST BE IN BETWEEN THE TWO LETTERS.
?
FOLLOW ME! WE HAVE TO FIND THE WAY TO THE SECOND "A." I KNOW THE WAY OUT ONCE WE GET THERE.
YES, MAYBE...
THE WAY OUT... OH MY, OH MY... I'D HAVE BEEN BETTER OFF STAYING ON MY ISLAND, WITH ALL THE COMFORTS OF HOME, MY MAN FRIDAY, AND ALL THE REST...
BRRROOM
QUICK! IT'S GOING TO CRUSH US!
THE C-C-C-C-C-C-CARPET!

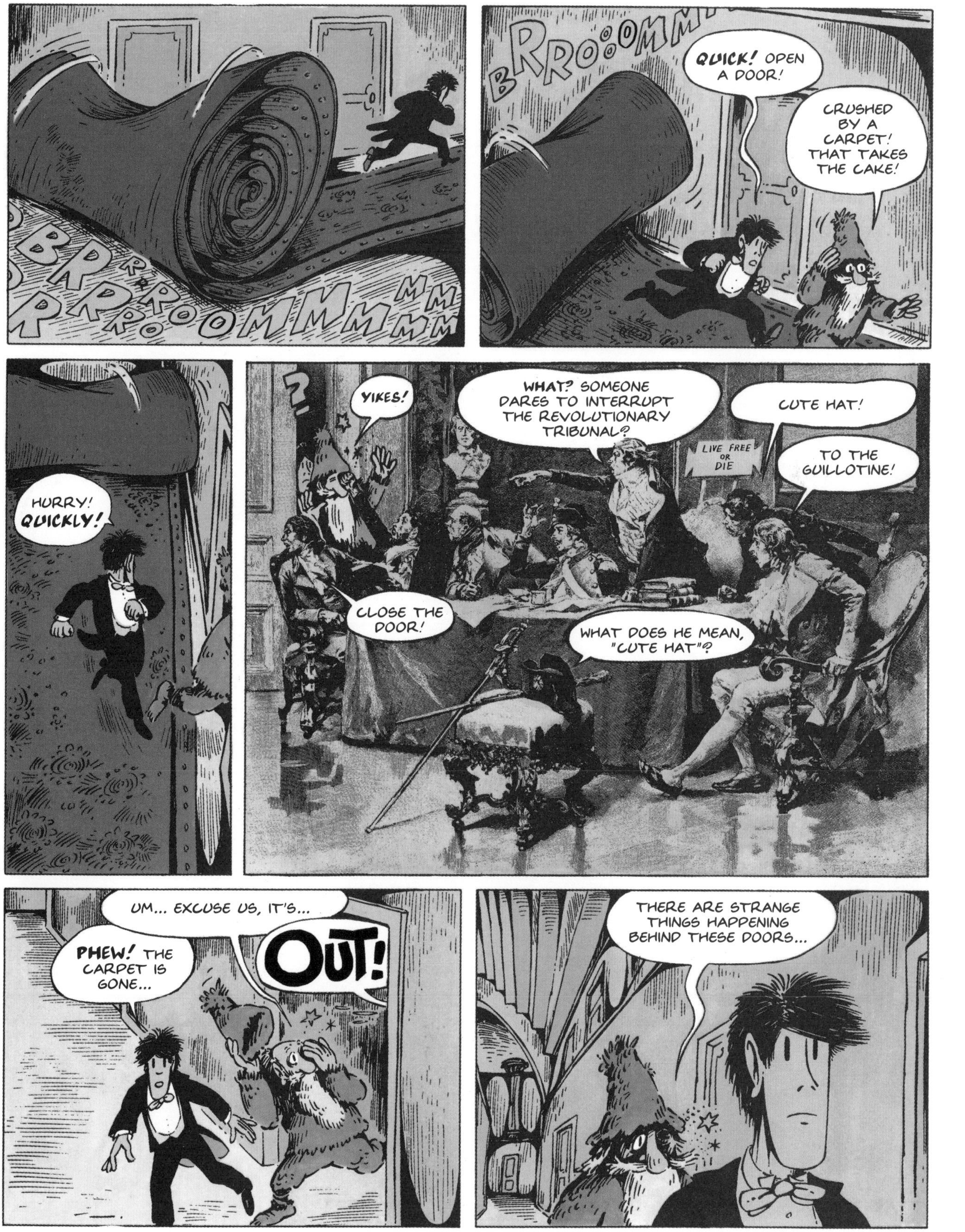
QUICK! OPEN A DOOR!
CRUSHED BY A CARPET! THAT TAKES THE CAKE!
HURRY! QUICKLY!
YIKES!
WHAT? SOMEONE DARES TO INTERRUPT THE REVOLUTIONARY TRIBUNAL?
CUTE HAT!
LIVE FREE OR DIE
TO THE GUILLOTINE!
CLOSE THE DOOR!
WHAT DOES HE MEAN, "CUTE HAT"?
UM... EXCUSE US, IT'S...
PHEW! THE CARPET IS GONE...
OUT!
THERE ARE STRANGE THINGS HAPPENING BEHIND THESE DOORS...

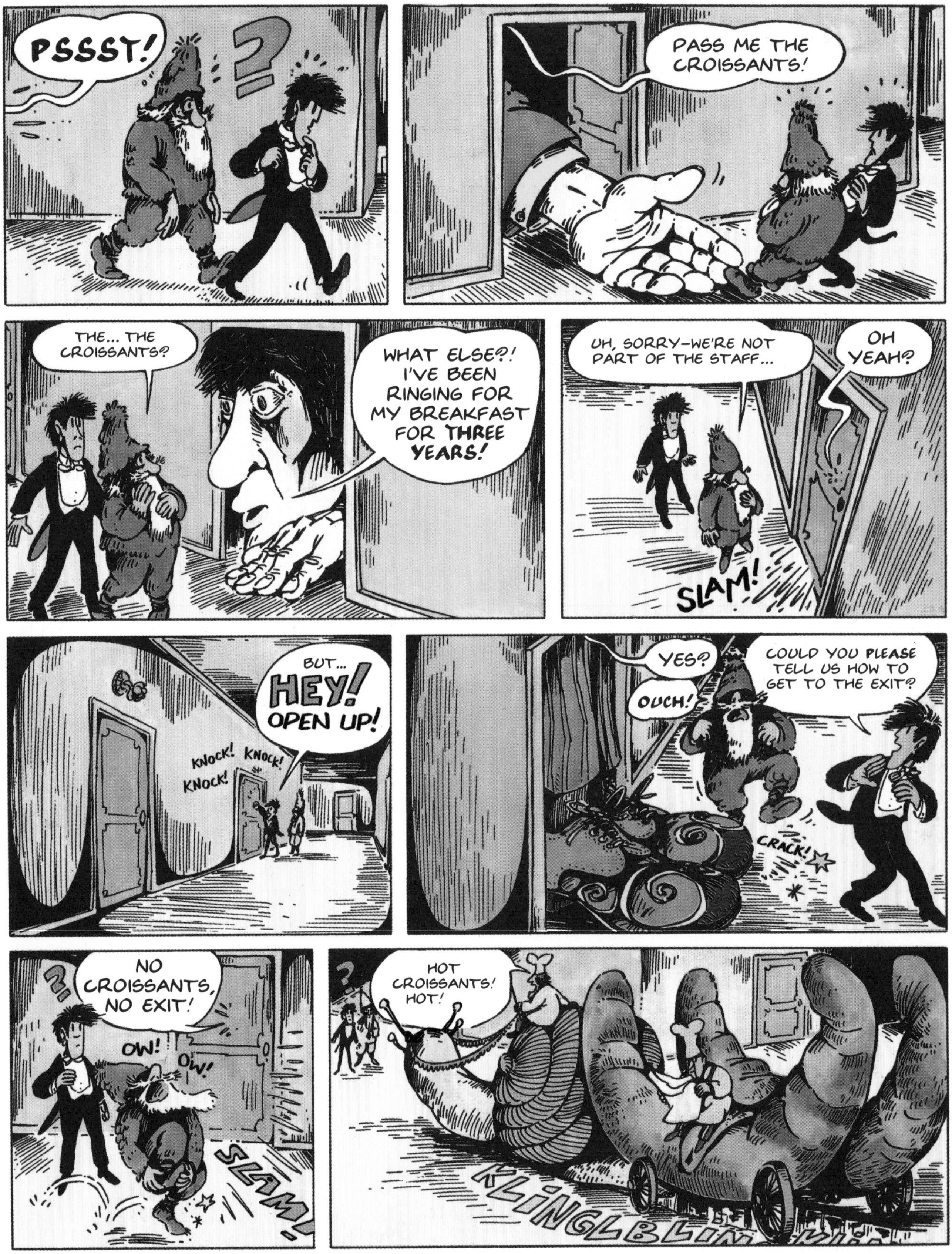
PSSST!
?
PASS ME THE CROISSANTS!
THE... THE CROISSANTS?
WHAT ELSE?! I'VE BEEN RINGING FOR MY BREAKFAST FOR THREE YEARS!
UH, SORRY—WE'RE NOT PART OF THE STAFF...
OH YEAH?
SLAM!
BUT... HEY! OPEN UP!
KNOCK! KNOCK! KNOCK!
YES?
OUCH!
COULD YOU PLEASE TELL US HOW TO GET TO THE EXIT?
CRACK!
NO CROISSANTS, NO EXIT!
OW! OW!
SLAM!
HOT CROISSANTS! HOT!

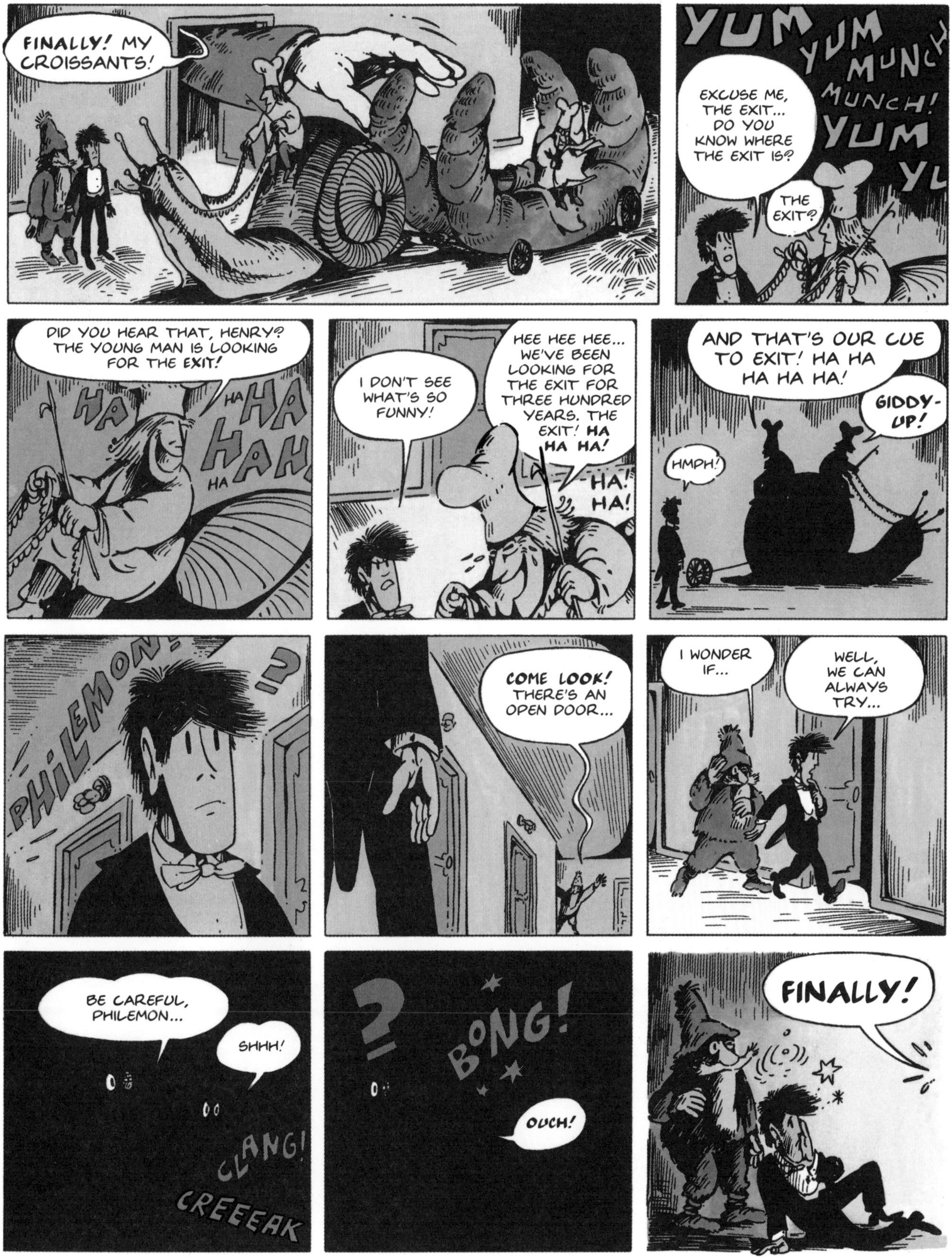
FINALLY! MY CROISSANTS!
YUM YUM MUNCH MUNCH! YUM YU
EXCUSE ME, THE EXIT... DO YOU KNOW WHERE THE EXIT IS?
THE EXIT?
DID YOU HEAR THAT, HENRY? THE YOUNG MAN IS LOOKING FOR THE EXIT!
HA HA HA HA HAH HA
I DON'T SEE WHAT'S SO FUNNY!
HEE HEE HEE... WE'VE BEEN LOOKING FOR THE EXIT FOR THREE HUNDRED YEARS. THE EXIT! HA HA HA!
HA! HA!
AND THAT'S OUR CUE TO EXIT! HA HA HA HA HA!
GIDDY-UP!
HMPH!
PHILEMON!
?!
COME LOOK! THERE'S AN OPEN DOOR...
I WONDER IF...
WELL, WE CAN ALWAYS TRY...
BE CAREFUL, PHILEMON...
SHHH!
CLANG!
CREEEEAK
?
BONG!
OUCH!
FINALLY!

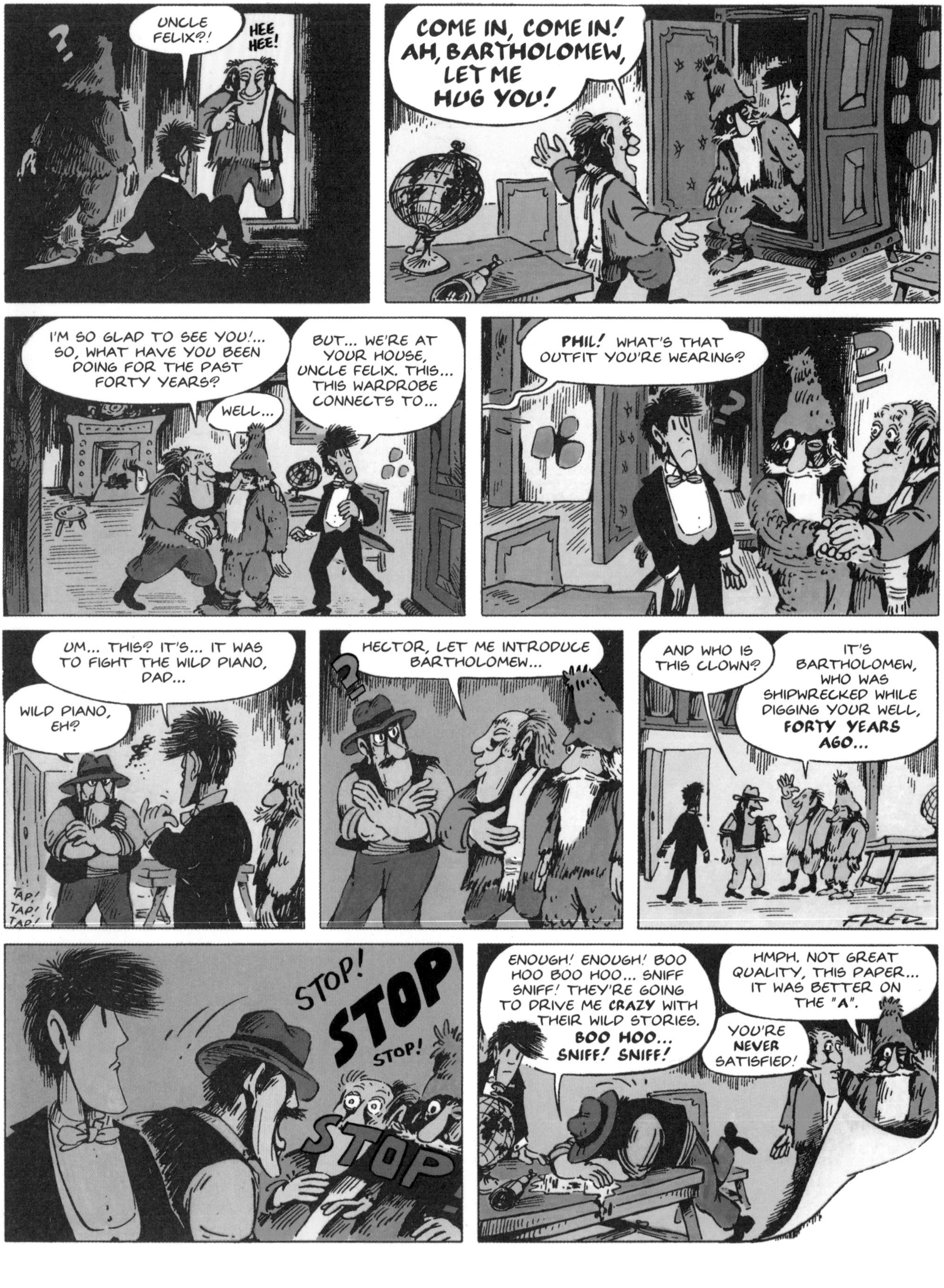
UNCLE FELIX?!
HEE HEE!
COME IN, COME IN! AH, BARTHOLOMEW, LET ME HUG YOU!
I'M SO GLAD TO SEE YOU!... SO, WHAT HAVE YOU BEEN DOING FOR THE PAST FORTY YEARS?
WELL...
BUT... WE'RE AT YOUR HOUSE, UNCLE FELIX. THIS... THIS WARDROBE CONNECTS TO...
PHIL! WHAT'S THAT OUTFIT YOU'RE WEARING?
UM... THIS? IT'S... IT WAS TO FIGHT THE WILD PIANO, DAD...
WILD PIANO, EH?
TAP! TAP! TAP!
HECTOR, LET ME INTRODUCE BARTHOLOMEW...
AND WHO IS THIS CLOWN?
IT'S BARTHOLOMEW, WHO WAS SHIPWRECKED WHILE DIGGING YOUR WELL, FORTY YEARS AGO...
FRED
STOP! STOP STOP! STOP
ENOUGH! ENOUGH! BOO HOO BOO HOO... SNIFF SNIFF! THEY'RE GOING TO DRIVE ME CRAZY WITH THEIR WILD STORIES. BOO HOO... SNIFF! SNIFF!
HMPH. NOT GREAT QUALITY, THIS PAPER... IT WAS BETTER ON THE "A".
YOU'RE NEVER SATISFIED!

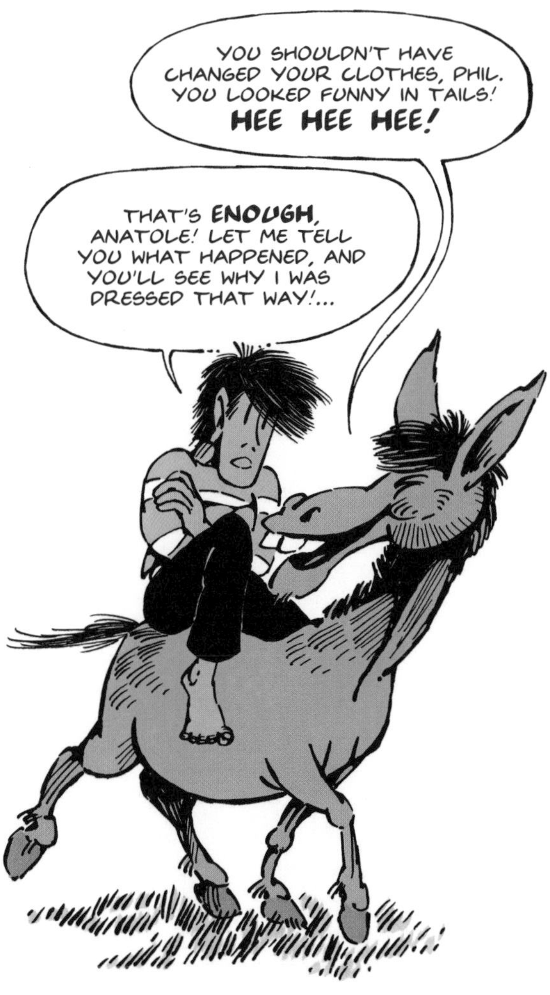
YOU SHOULDN'T HAVE CHANGED YOUR CLOTHES, PHIL. YOU LOOKED FUNNY IN TAILS! **HEE HEE HEE!**
THAT'S **ENOUGH**, ANATOLE! LET ME TELL YOU WHAT HAPPENED, AND YOU'LL SEE WHY I WAS DRESSED THAT WAY!...

Down the well, in a world of utter fantasy...

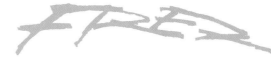

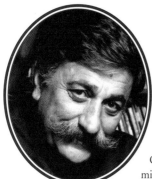

Frédéric Othon Aristidès (1931-2013), known as Fred, was one of France's most influential and revered cartoonists. Born in Paris to a Greek immigrant family, Fred encountered the myths and stories of many different countries. His mother first exposed him to British literature and, as he grew older, he started to read Edgar Allan Poe, Charles Dickens, and Oscar Wilde. In the sixties, Fred co-founded *Hara-Kiri*, the leading satirical publication of the May '68 movement–he designed its first 60 covers. Philémon, his story for young readers, was first published in *Pilote* in 1965 by René Goscinny, the author of the Astérix series. Philémon is Fred's most celebrated creation: millions of young French people have grown up with it, and it has inspired many of today's most talented cartoonists. The Philémon stories are densely populated with allusions to various literary and artistic sources, all woven together with Fred's unique absurdist logic. While there's no knowing where exactly he found this inspiration, Fred said he often got his best ideas while taking a bath.

Alice in Wonderland

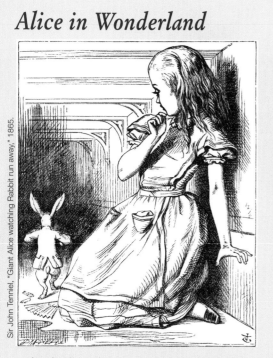

Sir John Tenniel, "Giant Alice watching Rabbit run away," 1865.

BUT AT LEAST LET ME EXPLAIN!
NOT A WORD! YOU MUSTN'T SPEAK IN THE PRESENCE OF A LAWYER!
QUIET!

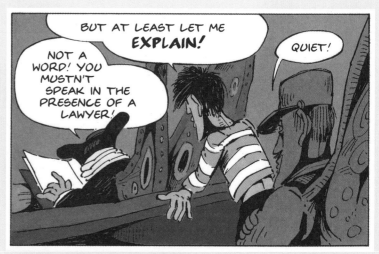

Lewis Carroll's influential fantasy novel *Alice's Adventures in Wonderland* was first published in 1865. In it, a young girl named Alice follows a rabbit down a rabbit hole, where she undergoes transformations and has many strange adventures with odd characters. *Alice in Wonderland*, as it is often called, plays with logic and turns it on its head. Alice takes part in the trial of the Knave of Hearts, which proceeds chaotically, with the Queen of Hearts asserting that the sentence should come before the verdict. The same lack of logic and inversion of reality are seen in Philemon's trial. His lawyer, who was not present at the supposed crime, is a witness against him, and there is a hostile, tyrannical judge, who blames Philemon when he smashes his own finger with his gavel.

OW!
BOOM!
ASSAULT AND BATTERY OF A MAGISTRATE. YOU'LL PAY FOR THIS!

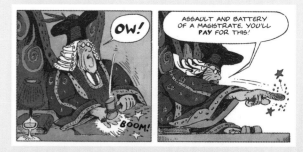

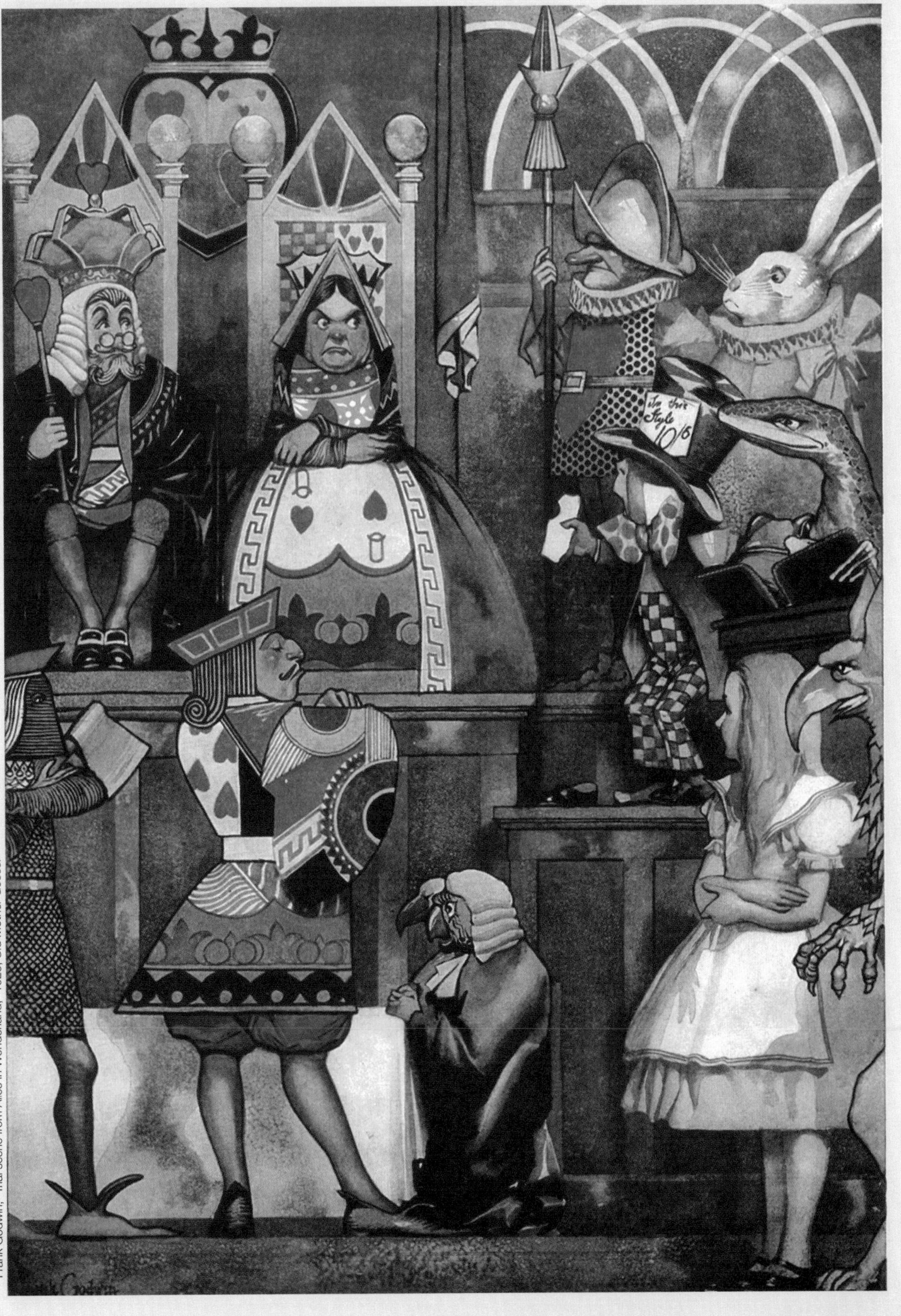
In this Style 10/6
Frank Godwin, "Trial scene from Alice in Wonderland," 1925, *Old Mother Goose.*

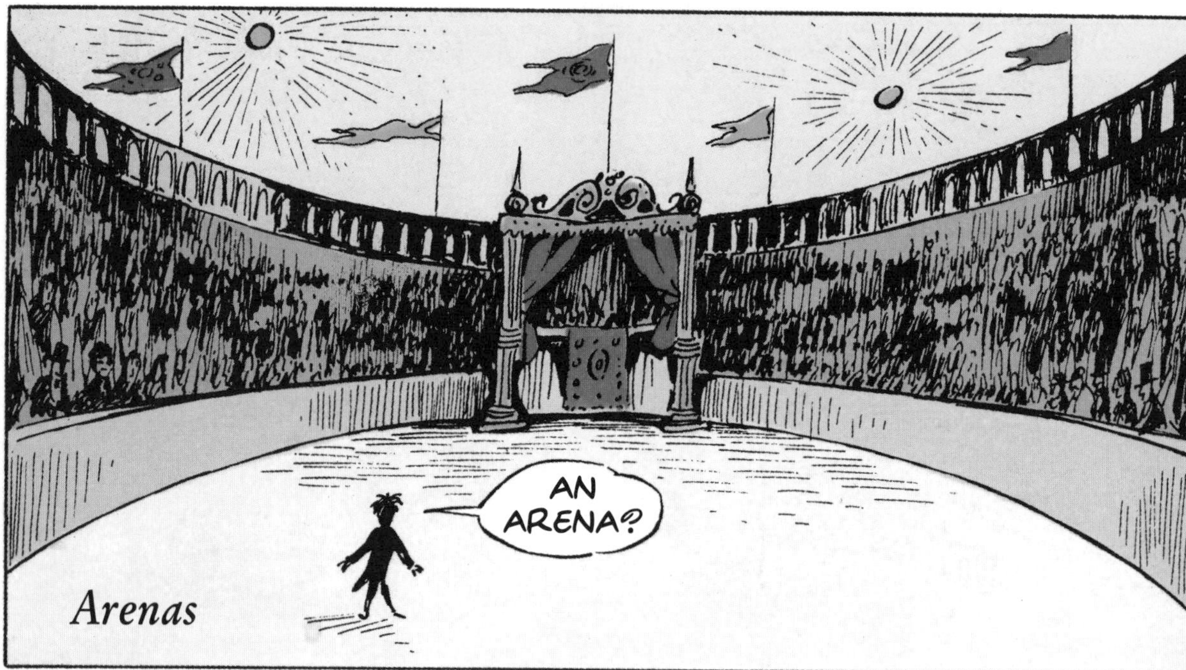
AN ARENA?

Arenas

The Ancient Greeks often attended plays in outdoor theaters, or amphitheaters (from *amphi*, meaning "around" and *theatron*, meaning "place for viewing"). The Romans adapted the Greek amphitheater into the "arena," which was used for a variety of forms of entertainment, including gladiatorial combats. The word arena comes from the Latin word *harena*, meaning "sand" or "sandy place," because sand was strewn on the floor to soak up the blood. These arenas, in turn, led to bullrings, where men (and a few women) fought against bulls, doing all kinds of fancy moves, just like Philemon with the wild piano. If you look carefully, you can see that the wild piano has hooves like a bull. Many bullfights in Spain and southern France still take place in Roman amphitheaters. Modern-day sporting events, like football, take place in a kind of arena, also called a stadium.

Gulliver's Travels

The giant prisoner who has been waiting years for his croissants could be a reference to Lemuel Gulliver, the main character of *Gulliver's Travels*, by Jonathan Swift, published in 1726. Gulliver, like Philemon, loves

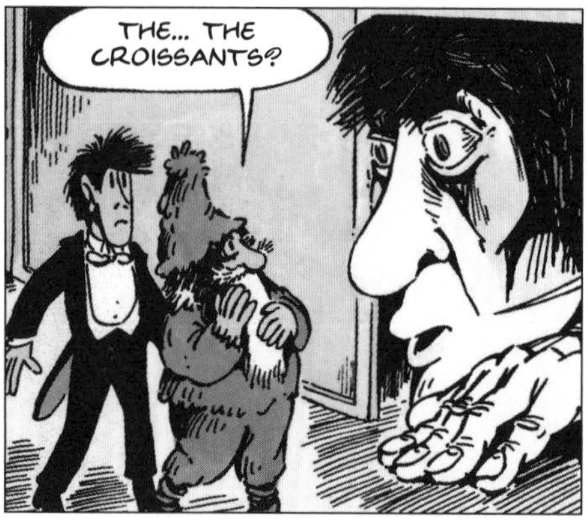
THE... THE CROISSANTS?

to travel. He finds himself prisoner to a race of tiny people in the island country of Lilliput. This is just the start of Gulliver's amazing adventures, however, which include time in the land of Brobdingnag, where people are twelve times as tall as humans, and a visit to the flying island of Laputa.

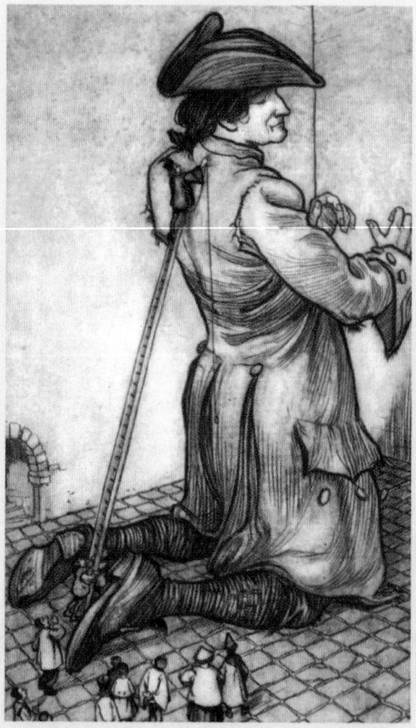
Arthur Rackham, "Lilliput," 1904, *Gulliver's Travels.*

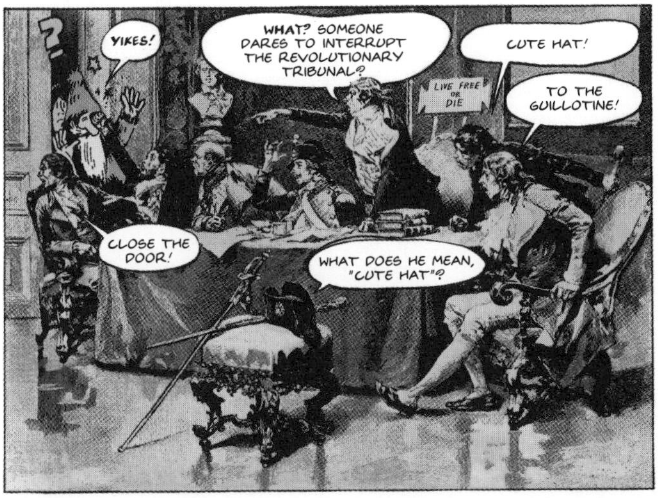
YIKES!
WHAT? SOMEONE DARES TO INTERRUPT THE REVOLUTIONARY TRIBUNAL?
CUTE HAT!
LIVE FREE OR DIE
TO THE GUILLOTINE!
CLOSE THE DOOR!
WHAT DOES HE MEAN, "CUTE HAT"?

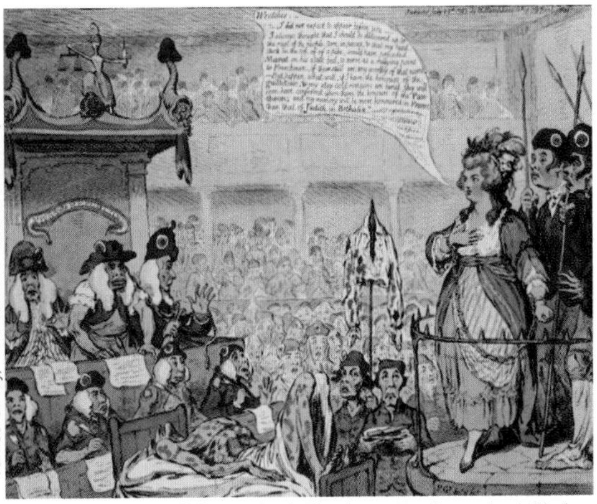

James Gillray, "The heroic Charlotte la Cordé," 1793.

An early cartoon of the trial of Charlotte Corday, who killed revolutionary leader Jean-Paul Marat.

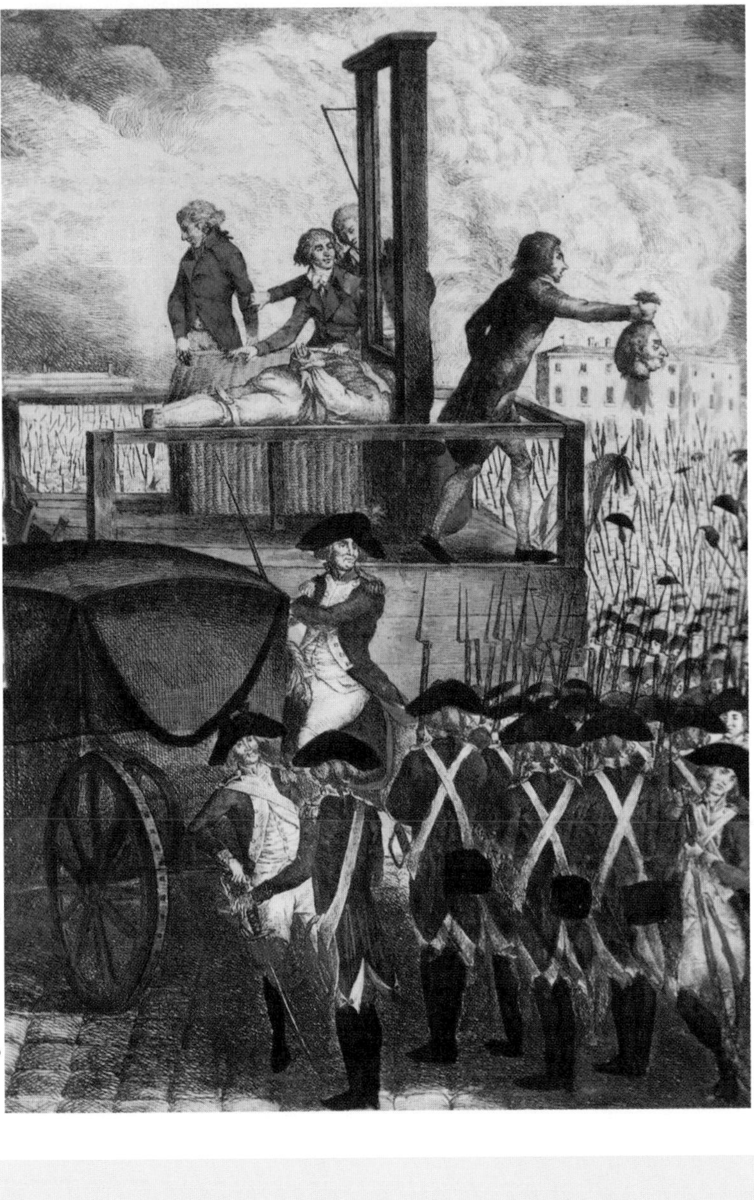

Georg Heinrich Sieveking, "The Execution of Louis XVI," 1793, *Engraving.*

The Revolutionary Tribunals

The French Revolution of 1789, in which the royal family was overthrown, was followed by a period of political violence and mass executions now known as the Reign of Terror. The Revolutionary Tribunal was first set up in 1792 for the trial of "enemies of the revolution," those who voiced their disagreement with the new ruling party. Prisoners could not have lawyers defend them or have witnesses speak on their behalf. Death was the only penalty, and there was no appeal. In less than three years, thousands were brought to trial and sent to the guillotine, a wooden machine set up in a public square. A large, heavy blade dropped down to chop off the head of the offender.

The Lion, the Witch and the Wardrobe

Philemon and Bartholomew get back home by coming through a wardrobe, an homage to the C. S. Lewis classic *The Lion, the Witch and the Wardrobe* (1950), the first of seven books of the Chronicles of Narnia. In Lewis's fantasy world, four children enter a wardrobe and find themselves in Narnia, a fantastic land of talking animals and mythical creatures ruled over by the White Witch. The children must save Narnia and their own lives, just as Philemon must save himself from the wild piano.

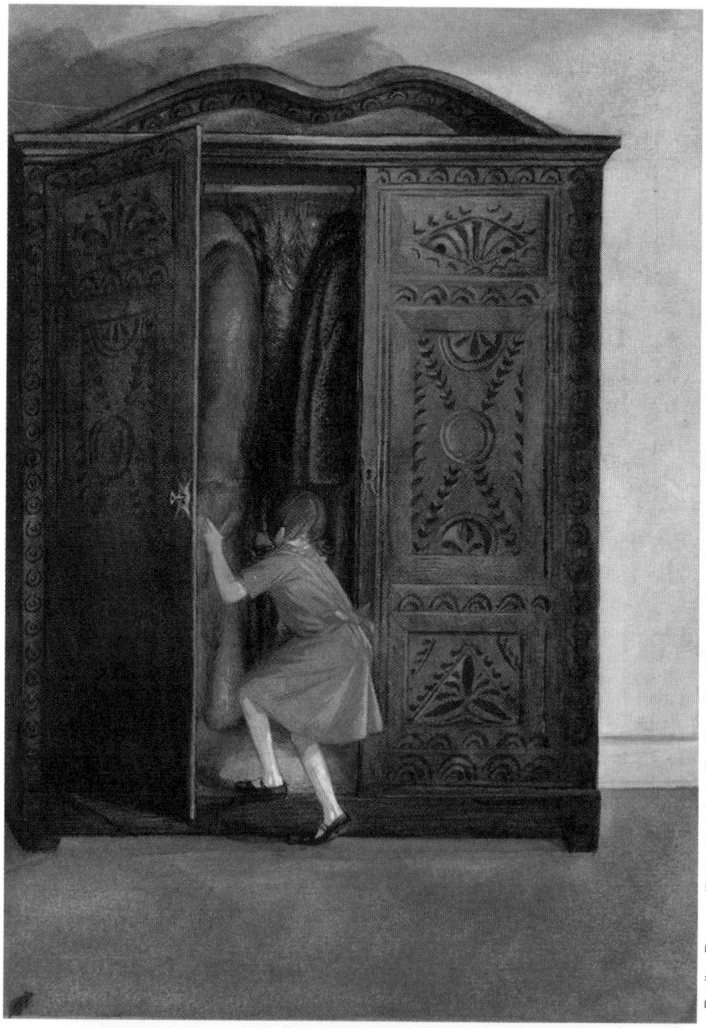

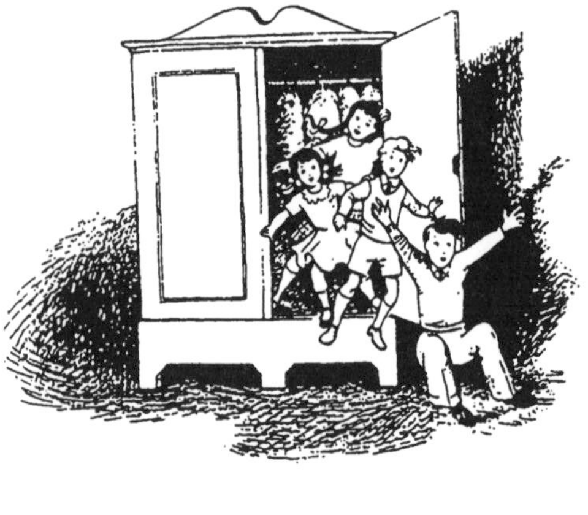

Pauline Baynes, Illustrations from *The Lion, The Witch, and the Wardrobe* © CS Lewis Pte Ltd 1950.

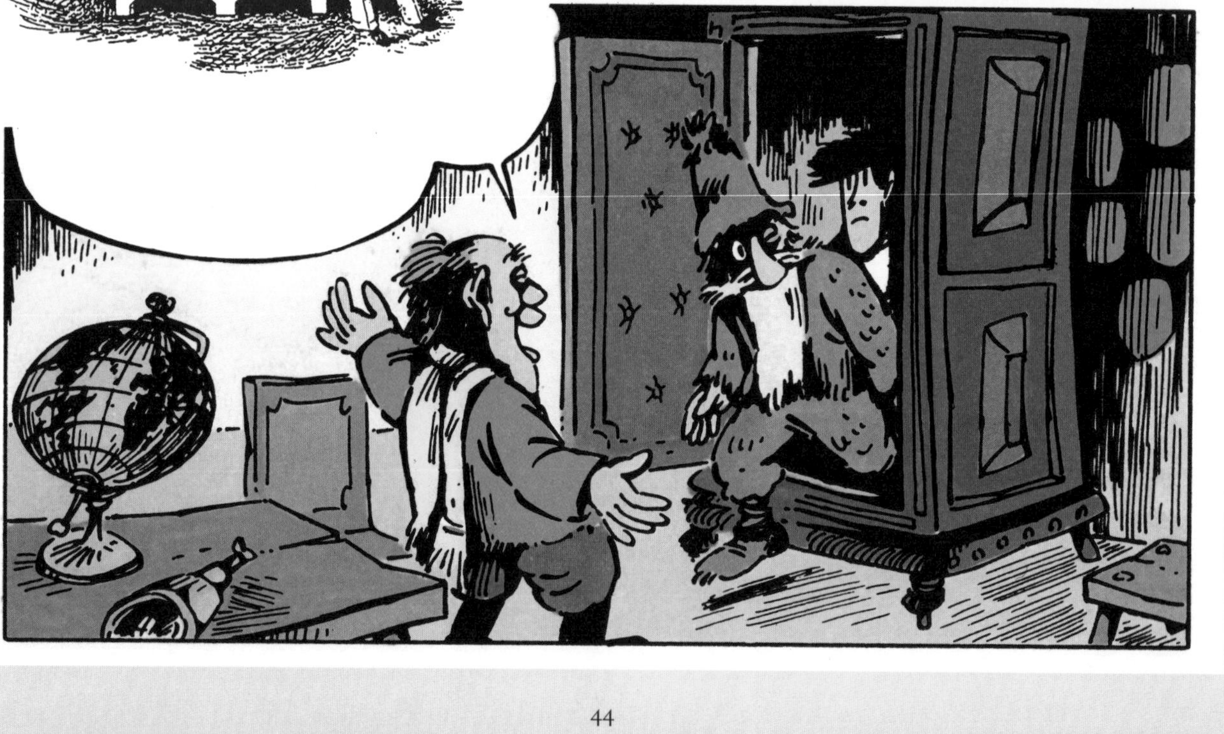

Winged Creatures

Winged people and creatures appear in stories and myths from around the world. In this book, humans grow butterfly wings. In world mythology, wings are usually a sign of magic, and resemble the wings of birds or butterflies.

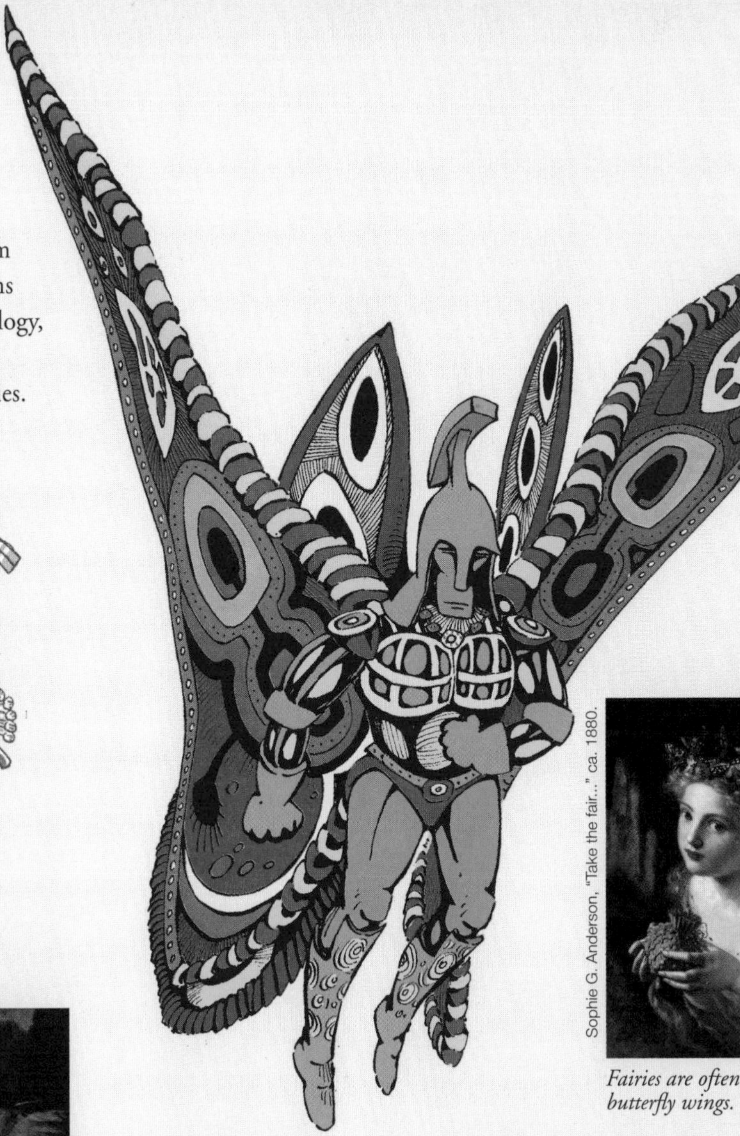

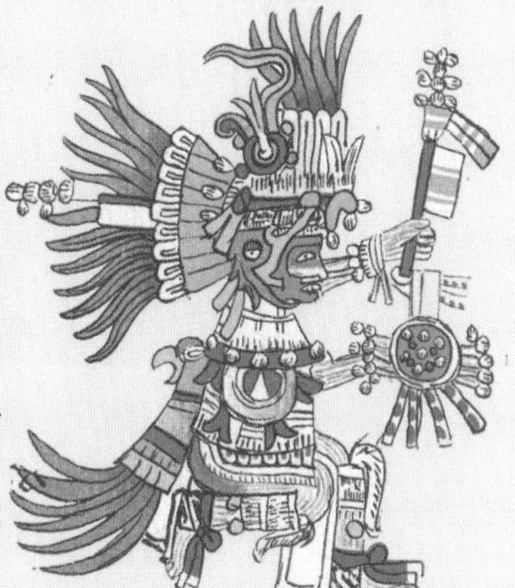

Sixteenth Century, *Codex Telleriano-Remensis.*

Huitzilopochtli, the Aztec god of war and the sun, is represented with hummingbird wings or feathers.

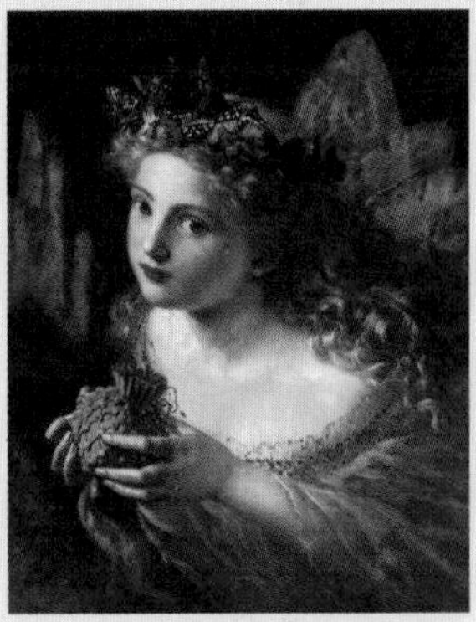

Sophie G. Anderson, "Take the fair..." ca. 1880.

Fairies are often portrayed with butterfly wings.

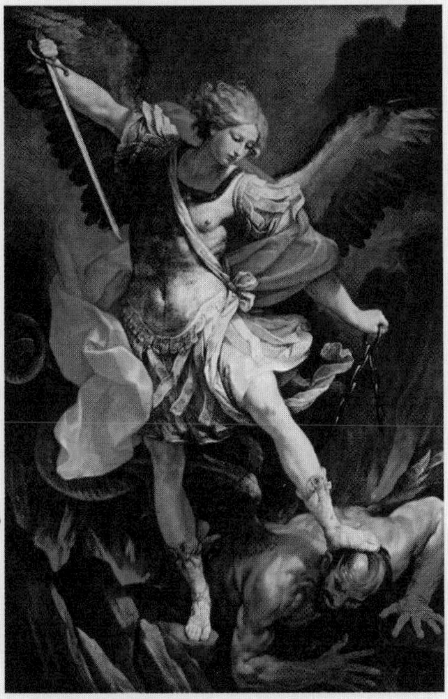

Guido Reni, "Archangel Michael," ca. 1636.

Angels are traditionally depicted with human form and feathered wings.

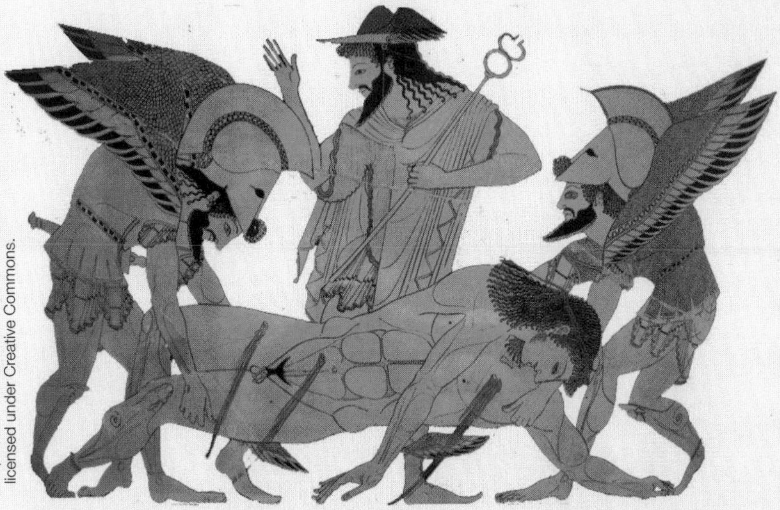

Euphronios, 515 BCE, *Euphronios Krater.* Photo by Jaime Ardiles-Arce, licensed under Creative Commons.

Thanatos, the winged Greek spirit of death. and his twin brother, Hypnos, the spirit of sleep, carry the dead to the underworld. Hermes, the god of transitions and the messenger between the mortal and divine, depicted in the center, has small wings on his ankles.

Tips for Parents, Teachers, and Librarians:

TOON GRAPHICS FOR VISUAL READERS

TOON Graphics are comics and visual narratives that bring the text to life in a way that captures young readers' imaginations and makes them want to read on—and read more. When the authors are also artists, they can convey their creative vision with pictures as well as words. They can enhance the overarching theme and present important details that are absorbed by the reader along with the text. Young readers also develop their aesthetic sense when they experience the relationship of text to picture in all its communicative power.

Reading TOON Graphics is a pleasure for all. Beginners and seasoned readers alike will sharpen both their literal and inferential reading skills.

Let the pictures tell the story

The very economy of comic books necessitates the use of a reader's imaginative powers. In comics, the images often imply rather than tell outright. Readers must learn to make connections between events to complete the narrative, helping them build their ability to visualize and to make "mental maps."

A comic book also gives readers a great deal of visual context that can be used to investigate the thinking behind the characters' choices.

Pay attention to the artist's choices

Look carefully at the artwork: it offers a subtext that at first is sensed only on a subliminal level by the reader and encourages rereading. It creates a sense of continuity for the action, and it can tell you about the art, architecture, and clothing of a specific time period. It may present the atmosphere, landscape, and flora and fauna of another time or of another part of the world. TOON Graphics can also present multiple points of view and simultaneous events in a manner not permitted by linear written narration. Facial expressions and body language reveal subtle aspects of characters' personalities beyond what can be expressed by words.

Read and reread!

Readers can compare comic book artists' styles and evaluate how different authors get their point across in different ways. In investigating the author's choices, a young reader begins to gain a sense of how all literary and art forms can be used to convey the author's central ideas.

The world of TOON Graphics and of comic book art is rich and varied. Making meaning out of reading with the aid of visuals may be the best way to become a lifelong reader, one who knows how to read for pleasure and for information—a reader who *loves* to read.

World map courtesy of the National Geographic Society

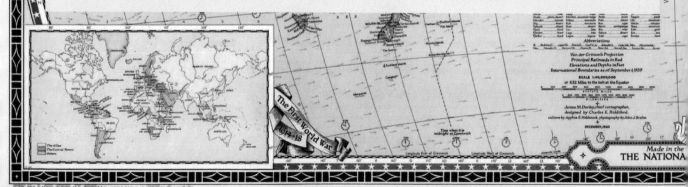